INCONVENIENT *love*

KATRINA MARIE

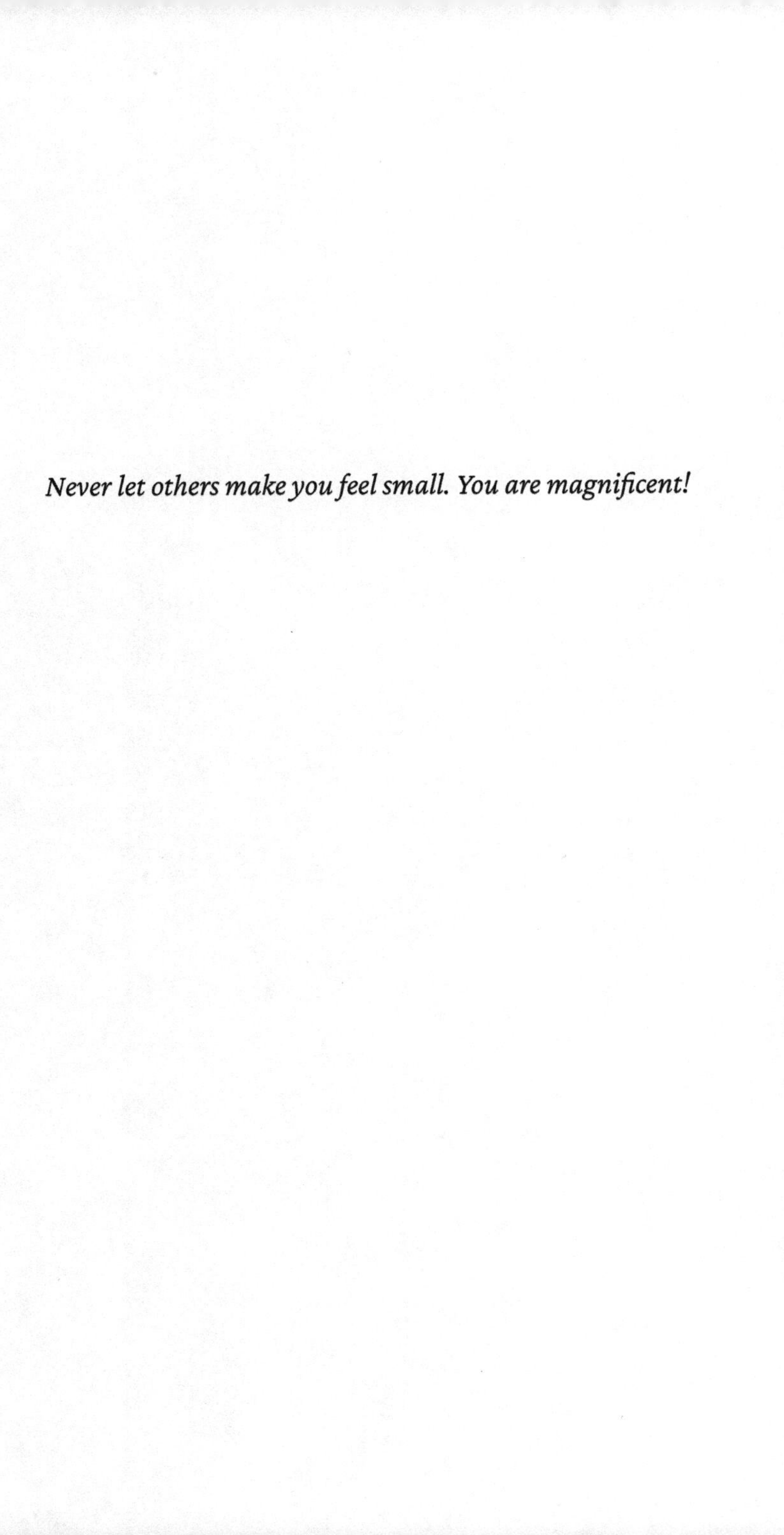

Never let others make you feel small. You are magnificent!

prologue

GRADUATION NIGHT IS ALWAYS BITTERSWEET. With my business degree in hand, I'm expected to head out into the big wide world and be a functioning adult. Hell, I've barely managed to get through my college years.

"Kate, are we going to that party tonight?" Samantha, one of my best friends, calls out from across pathway. Our other friend, Emily, stands beside her, shaking her head.

I glance at my parents and their eyes narrow. "Probably not. I need to finish packing." Immediately after the words are out, I mouth "yes" to her.

It's a bad idea, I know it to my very core. Parties are the reason I barely made it through college. Of course, I studied, but never until the last minute. Luckily, Emily's parents aren't around because they would make a whole scene. It's a wonder they allowed her to be friends with us in high school. The only one missing is Caroline, but she was so wrapped up in her high school sweetheart that she went to college where he was accepted. I don't fault her. You have to follow your heart, I guess.

But the last thing I need is some guy telling me what to do, and what's acceptable. I see enough of that with my parents and it's not the life I want for me. I'm not immune to the words some of my fellow classmates have called me while here, but I don't care. We only have one life. Why not enjoy it however we want?

"Are you coming home tomorrow?" My dad's voice can barely be heard over the chatter surrounding us. Parents doting over the accomplishments of their kids almost drown him out.

"It'll probably be Sunday or Monday." I turn toward him, so he knows I'm listening.

"Why so long?" Mom frowns. I swear it doesn't matter what I tell them, they will always have something to disapprove of.

"I have to get everything packed up and clean my dorm before I head back."

I know it's the right answer when she drops the subject. If it wasn't fine, she would have come back with some remark. Honestly, I'm surprised she didn't offer to help me just so I'd come home sooner. All I know is the first thing I plan on doing when I get home is look for an apartment. There's no way I can live with my parents. They aren't horrible, but they are overbearing. More than I think most parents, except maybe Emily's.

"We'll let you get to it, then," Dad wraps an arm around my shoulder for a quick hug, "call us when you're on your way."

"I will."

"We're proud of you." He gives me one more squeeze and releases me to my mom.

Her arms go around me and her grip is so tight it's hard to breathe. "You've done great, sweetheart. I can't wait to see what you will accomplish."

"Thanks, Mom. But couldn't you show less strength?"

"Oh, sorry," she tucks a piece of hair behind her ear. "We'll see you when you get home. Love you."

"Love you, too."

Finally, they walk away. My focus stays on their backs until they are nearing the doors to exit the stadium. The college is close enough to Asheville that they'll go home, thank God. The last thing I need is for them to get a hotel and pop in unannounced.

"I didn't think they were ever going to leave," Samantha throws an arm over my shoulder. "I think they may have been more overprotective than Emily's parents."

"That's because her parents know she's going to be just fine," I nod toward our friend in question as she joins us, "mine are probably wondering how the hell I made it out of high school."

"Why? It's not like we were bad...well, not entirely." Sam grins. That is a massive understatement. If our parents only knew how much we skipped school, or stayed out all night, they'd be freaking out. Hell, they probably would have never let us leave for college.

"If I remember," Emily clears her throat, "I was the one who kept y'all out of serious trouble."

"Well, you and Caroline," Sam adds, "y'all were our voice of reason most of the time."

"Do either of you know what you're going to do when we get back?" It's a small fear that has been playing in the back of my mind for a while. What if after all this I'm still a failure? I'd just be proving my parents correct.

"I thought we were doing the flower shop thing?" Samantha stares at me as if I've lost my mind.

"Yeah, but it's not like any of us can afford to buy a space for it."

"We don't have to buy the space just yet," Emily adds. "We only need to lease a small space until we grow."

"I don't think we have enough for that either." All the plans we've been making since high school seem to be unattainable, and I don't have a backup plan. Sam and Emily will be fine. They are able to swerve into a new lane when they need to. But me...I can't do that. With my personal life, yes. But with something like be an actual adult, I don't know that I'm built for it.

"You're making tomorrow's problem a today problem," Sam bumps into me, "we can talk about this once we get back to Asheville. For now, let's check out the parties on Greek Row. Everything else can wait. Tonight is our last night before we become functioning members of society. We need to live it up and go out with a bang."

"Literally," I smirk.

I loop my arms through each of theirs. Samantha is right, we can figure everything else out when we get back home. For now, we need to go out and live our best life.

CHAPTER ONE

"THERE'S no way we're going to make all this happen." Samantha, Emily, and Caroline are hovering over my shoulder while we look over the calendar for the next month. "How are we supposed to get all these flowers to where they need to be? Get the staging set up for the weddings on the schedule? And keep the shop open?"

This is something we've always wanted to do. A dream since high school and we took flower arrangement classes. We only took it because we thought it would be a blowoff class. Little did we know how much we'd enjoy it. Now...we can barely keep up with arrangement orders.

"We may have to start saying no to some jobs," Caroline sighs before walking around the desk to sit in one of the chairs in front of it. "If we can't keep up, we'll eventually screw up an order and lose business. Your brother taking care of deliveries helps, but it's not enough."

"Thanks for the support," Kai, my brother comes into the office, "you're not wrong, though."

"This is what happens when the friends of one of the biggest indie rock groups says they want to use you for their arrangements," Sam laughs. "We haven't even done the wedding and people have been emailing nonstop wanting to get on our schedule."

"Maybe you should know less influential people." Kai leans against the door with his arms across his chest. Why is my brother so freaking annoying?

"That would defeat the purpose of business growth," Emily argues. "I figured you would know that since you come from the business world."

"Yes, but you have to be able to sustain it."

"That's not possible right now." I bury my face in my hands. Never in my wildest dreams did I think we'd have this level of success in our tiny hometown, especially when we're fairly close to Dallas.

"Hiring more people would be a start," Caroline chimes in. "We'll need delivery drivers, folks to run the shop when we have appointments with clients, and an office manager."

"Why an office manager?" I lift my head up waiting for her to respond.

"So, we don't have so much on our plates." Her phone lights up and she glances it. No doubt it's her son or boyfriend wondering where she is. "We can't do all the things all the time. It'll give us more time to focus on what we do best. Making the arrangements and making sure our customers are happy."

"She has a point, Sis," Kai grins and raises his hand, "I call dibs on office manager."

All four of us whip our heads toward him. "Why do you think you'll automatically get the position? This isn't a board game where you can call what piece you're going to use." Emily lifts an eyebrow.

"Come on," he groans, "I've been doing the deliveries for over a month. Besides, this is literally what I did before I moved home. It only makes sense I should be in the hat for the job."

"We'll see." I'm quick to answer otherwise it'll turn into a huge debate, and I know Caroline wants to get home to her family.

"That's better than no." Kai grins and leaves the office. I swear he comes in here to disrupt everything just like he did when we were kids. He's always been the golden child, though. He also usually gets what he wants. A part of me wants to tell him no on that basis alone.

"He's so annoying. Can someone tell me why we thought it was a good idea to hire him?" Sam leans against the wall.

"Because we needed his help at the time. Then he just kind of stuck around." It's not like I asked them their thoughts when I offered the job to him. I just know we had to get out of the bind we were in with scheduling. He wasn't doing anything, and it made sense at the time.

"Yeah, kind of like mold," Emily scrunches her nose. "I swear he always does things to drive us bananas."

"That's kind of what little brothers do," Caroline laughs, "and I have two of them. It's never-ending."

"I don't know how you survived it. Most days I want to strangle Kai." I shake my head at all the times he's done something to purposely be a jerk, "especially when he was sleeping on my couch because he didn't want our mom to know he was home yet."

"At least y'all have that in common." Sam shifts against the wall.

"What?"

"Not wanting to deal with your overbearing mom."

"She's not as bad as she used to be." It's partially true. She still tries to dig her nails into anything and everything she can when it comes to me, but she's happy that I've ended up successful. She had her doubts about our business plans to say the least.

"True, but she still scares me. That's something I never expected from anyone's parents other than my own." Emily shivers at the thought.

Closing out of the calendar, I begin shutting down the computer. "I think that's enough for tonight. I know y'all have things to do and it's not our weekly girls' night. What do you say we meet back here first thing in the morning and post job listings."

All three of them murmur their agreement before heading toward the office door. "Quick question, are we really considering Kai for the office manager position?" Emily hovers just before the door while I gather my things.

Sam shrugs her shoulders, "He's the best option. He

already knows how we run things, and he has experience. I'm sure he'll be happy to have normal hours so he can see his girlfriend more often."

She's right. It's the best option for now. "We'll talk about it in the morning. He's definitely going to want a raise."

"Well," Caroline turns off the light as I make my way toward them, "as long as we keep booking these high-end events, it won't be a problem."

"That's enough business talk for the night," I push them out and close the door behind me, "y'all have a good night. I'll finish locking up."

"We can help." Emily offers.

"It's fine. I can do it." Little do they know I'll be stopping by Out of the Ashes on my way home. I need to blow off some steam before we tackle the hiring process in the morning. All this business has really cut into my personal time. I can't even remember the last time I entertained the thought of meeting up with someone. "Night, y'all."

I watch them head out the back door before making sure everything up front is closed ready for in the morning. As much as I love our company, it's draining. A night out is exactly what I need. I only hope the kitchen is still open because I'm starving.

The music is thumping through the walls and people are dancing around the table I'm sitting at. I'll join them soon enough, but I need a few drinks before to shake away the tension from the day. Maybe I should ask Angie how she handled the growth of the bar. Out of the Ashes used to be different. It was a hole in the wall bar that didn't have much clientele. That all changed when she became friends with an old classmate's girlfriend. Stella has turned this place around for the better and turned it into an experience.

"Hey, Trouble, you need another drink?" Eric, one of the bartenders takes the seat in front of me. "Where's the rest of your crew?"

"At home. It's not our usual night, you know that." I take a sip from my margarita, "but another drink would be great."

"You look...defeated. Anything I can help with?" He leans his elbows on the table ready to listen to whatever I'm going to tell him.

"Not really. Just work stuff."

"Y'all are getting big for a hometown floral business."

"That's part of it." How in the hell is he always so intuitive? He seems to have a pulse on whatever his patrons are going through. It's no wonder the new bartender fell for him.

"Well, if there's any way I can help, other than bring you more drinks, let me know." He stands up and pushes the chair in. The legs screeching across the hardwood floor is drowned out by the music.

"Not unless you want to work a second job by chance." I grin up at him as he shakes his head and walks away. It's the response I knew I was going to get, but he offered to help.

One of the waitstaff brings my next margarita and sets it on the table in front of me. Perfect timing since this one is almost gone. Honestly, it's going down a little too easily. Even though I walked here from the shop, I should probably slow down a bit after the next one. My apartment isn't too far away either, so the walk isn't terrible, but it's less fun when I'm tipsy. Usually, Emily or Caroline drive me home.

One last sip from the glass finishes it off, and I set it down next to the newly replaced one. I take a deep breath and push away the stress from the day. Whatever happens, we'll handle it. Growth is good, and I need to look at it with that mindset. Hopefully it helps.

I watch the crowd in front of me and think back to my college days. Sam, Emily, and I would hit the clubs, living our best life. I'm lucky to be able to work with my best friends and make a living doing it. Ugh, all these maudlin thoughts need to go right out the window.

Grabbing the fresh margarita, I take a drink. The sides of the glass are wet from the condensation, and I pick up the small napkin to wipe it off. The chair Eric vacated a few minutes ago moves. I swear he thinks he has to take care of everyone. "Eric, I wasn't play—"

My eyes move from the glass in my hand to the person who isn't Eric sitting in the chair. What the hell? This is so random. Who comes and just plops themselves into a seat at a stranger's table? Well, I guess I can't really fault them.

I've done the same thing on numerous occasions. And it was usually some guy I ended up going home with. It's just weird having the same thing happen to me. This is new.

"Um, who are you?" Hopefully that wasn't rude, but like who is this guy.

"Xander." He holds his hand out. His dark brown eyes twinkle in the dim lighting as he smirks. "You looked lonely."

Oh. My. God. "Does that pickup line usually work?" I grasp his hand and shake it lightly before pulling back.

He shrugs and leans back in his chair. "Sometimes. I mean, it's got about an eighty percent chance of it, anyway."

At least he's being honest. Not many people would be, especially when they are trying to pick someone up from the bar. "Let me guess, you were standing over there, and you saw me sitting alone minding my own business. You decided to come over and really thought those words were the ones that would endear me to you."

That may have been a tad bit bitchy, but it's really hard to be in the mood to play games. As much as I try to shake off the worries I have about the shop, it's just not working.

"Actually," he leans forward, elbows on the table, "I noticed you when you walked in. I was going to come over sooner, but then that guy sat down," he pauses to take a sip of his beer. "For a second, I thought he was your boyfriend or something. Then I saw him walk behind the bar and tell one of the waiters to bring you a drink. After that, I spent a few moments talking myself into coming over here."

"How does him going behind the bar equate to him not being my boyfriend? For all you know he is." I'm interested in what he has to say about this revelation.

He studies the margarita in my hand for a few seconds, and glances toward the bar. No doubt to the guy in question. "Well, mostly because he watches you like an overprotective brother, and he's staring at me like he wants to break my jaw. If he was your boyfriend, I probably wouldn't be in this fine establishment much longer."

"Oh." It's so weird being on this side of the conversation. It's usually me approaching men. Confidence isn't something I've ever had a problem with. But this...it's knocking me back a few steps. I have no idea what to do from here. At this point I've usually talked them into buying me a drink before we head off to be alone.

"Am I right?"

"Well, you're not wrong." Seriously, Kate, pull yourself together. I take a long pull from my drink. It feels like half of the drink is gone when I'm done. It takes everything in me not to throw my hands to my head from the rush of the drink. Something else that isn't typical of something I do. Slamming drinks ended in my early twenties.

"Want to dance?" He scoots the chair back and stands. His hand held out to me, waiting for me to take the leap.

xander

INDECISION FLASHES across her face as she struggles with the decision to join me on the dance floor. I have a feeling this isn't something she's used to. Maybe she doesn't come to bars often. Admittedly, even though I live in Asheville, this is the first time I've been to this bar. I usually go with my friends to Dallas and hit the clubs there. Tonight, though, I needed something a little more low-key. Turns out it seems like it was a good idea.

"Maybe you could tell me your name? I mean, you know mine." There, that should ease her mind some. Then we wouldn't exactly be strangers.

"Oh, sorry, it's Kate." She throws back the rest of the drink and wipes her hand on the napkin she'd discarded on the table.

Kate glances up at me through her eyelashes and a small smile lifts the corners of her mouth. That small gesture seals the deal, and I know she's going to come with me. She lifts her hand and places it in mine.

Her hand tightens on mine as she gets out of her seat. She follows behind me as I lead her to the dance floor. There's a stage at the front of the room, but there isn't a band playing. I'm not sure how they are handling the music, but an upbeat song I've never heard is playing through the speakers.

It's obvious she knows it because she immediately starts dancing. Her hips swaying back and forth. She turns until her back is against my chest, grinding against me, making me wish we were anywhere but in this bar. It's not something my thoughts normally turn to. Tonight, I feel like living on the edge. It's the only reason I approached her to begin with, aside from how beautiful she is. Stepping outside of my comfort zone is the only thing I could think of to make this day slightly better.

Other people are moving around us, but I barely notice. My eyes are glued to the woman in front of me. And that's exactly what Kate is...a woman. She's not the college age girls I typically go for. Hell, I thought she'd shoot me down and tell me to leave when I sat down at her table.

My hands reach for her hips and breathe a sigh of relief when she doesn't push them away. Our bodies move in sync to the music without a care in the world. Both of us needing this release more than I think either of us know. I don't even know her, but I know whatever was bothering her before I asked her to dance has floated away as the beat of the music surrounds us.

The song changes to something a little slower and cozier. She turns around and wraps her arms around my neck. My hands moving from her hips to encircle her waist. Her head rests against my chest, and we sway gently to lyrics talking about new love and the happiness found there. Love isn't what I'm looking for. She looks like she's at peace, and I'm glad I can provide that for her. Even if we are strangers.

When the songs over, she grabs my hand and pulls me off the dance floor. That's not what I expected. I mean, I didn't think she'd want to stay out there all night, but after two songs she's ready to toss me aside.

To my surprise, she stops once we're clear of being jostled by the others dancing. Leaning on her tiptoes, her lips are inches from my ear. "Wanna get out of here?"

This was not how I expected this to go. I hoped, but I didn't really think it would happen. "Um, sure."

"Cool. Let me close out my tab, and we can head out."

"I need to do the same."

She pulls us to the bar and the guy I saw at her table earlier is settling her ticket. Someone else is taking care of mine, but we're close enough that I can hear their conversation.

"Don't you think he's a little young for you?" I can feel his eyes on me.

"Hello, pot meet kettle," she laughs before adding, "I am perfectly capable of taking care of myself, Eric. And I didn't think this would bother you so much. There's a bigger age difference between you and Joan, right?"

"This is different."

"No, it's not." I see her sign her receipt out of the corner of my eye. She says something else to him, but I don't quite catch it.

The only two words I hear are "not serious" and that's a hard agree on my end. As attracted as I am to her, I don't need to jump into any sort of relationship. No, thank you.

Seconds later, she slips her hand into mine. "Let's get out of here. I hope you have a car because I walked here."

Oh shit. Where are we supposed to go? There's no way I can take her to my house. Not when I live with my parents.

Kate's place isn't too far. I'm also glad I have my car. Even though the weather isn't too bad, it's still pretty cold to be walking in. This winter has been mild compared to most. I'm honestly surprised she walked it to get to the bar.

I'm just happy she offered up her apartment. Trying to find an excuse not to go to mine was going to be a problem. Getting out of my parents' house has also become a top priority. It's so embarrassing in times like this. Not that it happens often.

"Are we going to sit in the car for the rest of the night? Or do you want to turn it off and go inside?" Kate puts her hand over mine on the gear shift.

My nerves have shot up now that she's put me on the

spot. In my head, I was smooth and could handle it. That's not how it seems to be playing out in actuality. "Definitely not sitting in the car."

Once I lift my hand up, she removes hers and I turn the car off. I push open the door and rush to her side of the car. Luckily, she hasn't made a move to open the door. This may be one night, or whatever, but it doesn't mean I can't act like a gentleman.

I pull open the car door and shiver. It got a lot colder out here than it was earlier, and even if we get upstairs and something goes terribly wrong, she didn't have to walk home in the cold. Holding out my hand to her, I wait for her to take it before helping out of her car.

"Thanks," her voice is a whisper on the breeze. I wonder if she's as nervous as I am. She seemed so confident when we left the bar, and seconds ago. Maybe she was hoping I'd provide a way out. The signals she sends are all over the place. Though, she's probably getting the same from me. She's out of me league. I knew that before I even approached her.

As soon as she's clear from the door, I close it before locking the car. "Lead the way."

To my surprise, she doesn't let go of my hand. She pulls me behind her and toward the staircase. The steps are narrow with wide gaps, and I almost lose my footing a couple of times as we go up. There are only four floors to the building, so I won't have to deal with those long no matter which floor she lives on.

On the third floor, she turns to the right, and I follow

along. Five doors down, she stops and pulls her keys out of her pocket. "Here we are."

"I bet it was a ton of fun moving in here." It's the only thing I can think to say to break the silence.

"It's going to be even more fun when I move out," she puts the key in the lock and turns. "I've acquired a lot more stuff, and I have a feeling my friends are going to hate me. Or they'll all of a sudden have plans."

She swings the door open and waits for me to get inside before closing it and turning on the lights. There's a small Christmas tree in the corner by the kitchen. The coffee table has various wedding magazines scattered across it.

Kate walks further into the apartment and tosses her keys on the table. "Don't mind the mess. I'm getting ideas for arrangements for work." She whirls on me and points her fingers, "and don't say anything about my tree. I haven't had a chance to put it away."

My hands go up in the air in surrender. "I wasn't going to say anything. Leave your tree up year-round. To each their own." I take a closer look at the magazines on the table. "What do you do for work?"

"I'm a florist." She moves between the couch and table, gathering the magazines and putting them in a pile. "My friends and I own a shop, and we've expanded our business to include weddings. It's kind of taken over everything."

"That sounds like a lot," she moves to straighten up something else, "you don't have to clean up because I'm here. It's fine."

Her shoulders relax. "Thanks. I'm not used to people coming over outside of my friends and family, and I don't really care what they think."

"I can go if you want." I point over my shoulder to the door.

"No, don't leave." Her words are rushed. She either needs to feel some sort of connection or let loose. I'll provide either for her.

Before I have a chance to say anything else her arms are around my neck and her mouth crashes into mine. She's giving me whiplash, but I don't argue. Both of us likely had the same intention when she asked me to come home with her.

The confident version of her I saw on the dance floor is back out in full force. Her hands move to the button of my jeans, unfastening them within seconds.

Pulling away from the kiss, I study her expression, ensuring this is what she wants. "Bedroom?"

She doesn't say anything for a moment before nodding her head toward the short hallway. "That way." She grabs my arm and pulls me in the direction she indicated. She doesn't bother closing the door once we're inside.

The room is dark, and the only light comes from the moon through the slats in the blinds. I move to turn on the lights, but she's already tugging me toward her bed. Her hands go to the bottom of my shirt, and she tugs until it's up and over my head.

"I, uh, don't have a condom." Stupid of me, of course. I usually always have one in my wallet. But I cleaned it out the other day, and I guess I forgot to put one back in there. It's not like I planned for this to be outcome for tonight, though. I only know I don't want to get a phone call in a few weeks to be told I'm going to be a dad. I'm not ready for that.

"No worries," Kate reaches into a nightstand and pulls out a foil square as she hands it to me and motions to my pants, "those need to come off."

By the time I have the pants off, and the condom rolled on, she's already completely undressed. "That was fast."

She shrugs her shoulders and pulls me toward her. "What can I say? I don't like to wait."

A part of me has a feeling she's done things like this a lot. No judgement here, but I'm used to taking my time. Hell, I like going slow. The more pleasure I can give the woman I'm with, the more it turns me on.

"I can see that." I press soft kisses along her shoulder, trying to slow the pace. She shifts her body until I'm between her and the bed. She captures my mouth and leans into me until I fall backwards. It's a miracle her lips never left mine with the sudden shift in movement. My hands are around her waist to keep her steady.

Her legs straddle my hips, and she runs a finger along my arm until she reaches one of my hands. She guides it between her legs and moans as I slip a finger inside. This isn't how I usually start foreplay, but I'm shocked by how much it turns me on. My dick twitches with every pump of my fingers and her gasps into my mouth.

One of her hands is on my shoulder and the other is

tracing a line along my chest and down. Without warning, her hand encircles my dick and I buck at the contact. Holy shit. This woman really knows what she wants. She shifts her body until she's over me, and I remove my hand, placing it on her hip.

She slides down slow and steady before rocking back and forth. Her breathing picks up speed and she breaks the kiss. Her long light brown hair is a curtain around us, her eyes focused on me, watching my reaction. Bending down, she kisses along my jawline, and I wrap my hands in her hair.

The rocking intensifies and I'm going to come before she has. Something that I swear hasn't happened to me before. At least, not to my knowledge. I feel her tighten around me and I can't hold back any longer. Gripping her hair tighter, I lift her face until my mouth meets hers. Letting our kiss swallow my moans of pleasure. I'm not sure how thin her walls are, and I don't want to be the reason a neighbor gets pissed off.

She deepens the kiss, our tongues twirling as she rocks into me one, two, three more times and I know she's orgasmed. She pulls her mouth from mine and collapses on top of me.

"Thank you." She whispers against me chest.

"Actually, I should be thanking you." I grin into the darkness.

She slides off of me. "I'm gonna go clean up. There's another bathroom in the hall."

"Okay." I watch her walk to the bathroom connected to her room before getting up to take care of the condom.

Kate has definitely rocked my world tonight. Despite the mixed feelings she kept throwing my way, she takes what she wants. It's something I can admire. But now, I don't know what happens next.

BRIGHT RAYS of light hit me in the face, and I sit straight up. Damn it, what time is it? I glance at my phone on the nightstand and jump out of bed when I see it's after nine. "Fuck, I'm late."

Xander shifts in the bed, turning away from the windows. I can't believe I let him stay over last night. That defeats the whole purpose of a one-night stand. But he was sweet, and we ended up watching horrible informercials while drinking wine until later than I usually stay up.

I grab my robe off the hook on the back of my door before heading to the other side of the bed. I push his shoulder until he wakes up. "Sorry to do this to you, but you need to go. I'm late for work."

"Oh," he rubs a hand down his face trying to get his bearings, "do you want me to drive you or anything?"

"No," I shake my head, "I still need to get ready and look somewhat decent."

"Okay," he throws the comforter off of him and finds his clothes on the floor, "I'll, um, see you around."

He's taking this pretty well. I haven't done the whole morning after conversation since I was in college. It never stops being awkward. "I'm sure you will."

I don't even bother making sure he leaves before I head to the bathroom and try to make myself presentable. A shower is out because I don't have the time. We're all supposed to be meeting about hiring folks this morning and I need to get to the shop as soon as possible.

Last night wasn't exactly a bad choice, but it definitely wasn't one I should have made. This is what happens when I get too in my feelings instead of thinking logically. The smart thing would have been to come home and binge watch TV. It's a little too late for should've, would've, could've though.

Now that I'm in a fresh set of clothes, I feel slightly better. Makeup isn't happening today. I grab my favorite gloss and shove it in my pocket before exiting my bedroom.

Xander is nowhere to be seen when I enter the living room. There is a corner of one of the magazines torn, though. What the hell? I know it wasn't like that last night. Grabbing my keys, I see the torn bit of paper next to them. A number is scrawled across with Xander's name printed on top.

I guess my shifting moods last night didn't scare him off. Not that I have any intention of calling him. Last night was fun, and that's all it was supposed to be. I leave the paper right where it is and head out the front door. If there is any luck on my side, somebody brought breakfast because I don't have time to stop. Especially since I'm walking. Maybe I should have let him drive me over.

⁂

"Well, well, well," my brother calls out as soon as I walk through the shop door. "Look who finally decided to show up."

"You don't have to be an ass, Kai." I argue. Today is the day I'm regretting letting him work here. "If you're going to be mean, please tell me, you at least have food."

"I didn't realize you could be bought so easily." He smirks and pushes over the box of pastries sitting on the cabinet.

"So, what did I miss?" Grabbing a jelly filled donut, I take a bit. The only thing that would make this better is a cup of coffee. I'm awake, but not completely.

Sam picks up a piece of paper. "We've made a list of the positions we need. At least three for the front counter, two drivers, and someone back here to help us with the arrangements. They'd have to be qualified, of course."

"Are two drivers enough?" One would think it is, but it usually takes all of us to get everything where it needs to go.

"That's all we have enough vans for," Caroline adds. "The only way to hire another driver would be if we bought another van. We could afford it, but I'm not sure if that's another expense we want to take on right now. At least not until we know how the weddings are going to pan out in the long run."

I take a few bites of my donut, thinking over everything they've laid out. It's a solid plan to begin with, and it's not like we have a choice. We badly need the help. It's the only way this shop is going to be a success. It's getting too big for the four of us to manage on our own, not counting my brother.

"Kai has already agreed to being the office manager." Emily shoots him a pointed stare. I swear sometimes you'd think they were siblings instead of me and him. "He's going to take care of the scheduling on all aspects, and the day-to-day stuff in the shop. We'll have one less thing to worry about. We're also going to start doing appointments with couples together instead of separately...at least as much as possible."

"I can get down with this," I grab a napkin and wipe off my hands, "will all of the calendars be synced? And is there any other software we need to use to make everything seamless?"

"I'm already on top of that, Sis," Kai points at his computer. "I'm getting everything set up now and will show y'all how to use it once it's done. In the meantime, I'm going to put out ads letting folks know we're hiring."

"Thanks." As annoying as he can be, he is very good at his job. He has the experience from his previous job before he moved home. I'm grateful he's willing to help us in making this business more amazing than it already is. "Oh, we'll also have to make sure there's enough room in the schedule for special events at the school. Almost everyone in town uses us."

"I'll make a note of it." The gleam in his eyes lets me know making him office manager is the right move. He did fine driving, but it's not where his passion truly lies. Doing all of this is what fuels him.

"I'm gonna go make a cup of coffee." I head toward the warehouse where we have a coffee pot tucked away in a corner. That's another thing I'd like to add when we have time. We need an actual break room for all these employees we're bringing in. Hell, we need it for us. It didn't seem important when we got enough money to buy the place instead of renting it. Now, it's ours and we need to make it feel that way.

"So, I heard an interesting tale this morning." I didn't realize Caroline followed me into the warehouse area.

"Oh yeah? And what was that?"

"It explains why you were in so late this morning." Caroline bumps into my shoulder.

Damn this town and their wagging tongues. "I'm not sure I know what you're talking about."

"Sure, you do," Sam adds from the other side.

"Did you really leave the bar with a younger guy last night?" Emily asks as she pulls another coffee pod out of the basket that holds them.

"Who told y'all that?" Either Caroline told them what she heard, or multiple people have been talking about it.

"Carlos." Caroline answers.

"He wasn't even working last night. How would he know?" It takes me all of two seconds to figure out how word got out. "I swear, I'm going to murder Eric. Why does he make it a point to get into everyone's business?"

"So, it's true then?" Emily moves aside as I turn away from the coffee pot so she can make hers. Caroline and Samantha also move out of my way.

They aren't going to leave me alone until I give them the details. "Yeah, it's true. It was completely unplanned."

"Aren't most one night stands not planned?" Sam laughs and follows me.

"Nobody likes a smart ass." Why are they on my case about this? They've never questioned what I do outside of work before. Besides, it's not like this is something out of the ordinary for me.

"Sorry." She doesn't sound like she is, but I let it slide. "It's just you usually don't do that here. And you didn't bother telling us about it first thing this morning. We had to hear about it from Caroline."

Well, at least I know it didn't come from a bunch of people talking. It was just Eric ratting me out to Carlos, who knew damn well he'd tell my friend.

"I was kind of in rush to get here after I slept through my alarm. I would have been here sooner if I would have let him drive me."

Emily gasps, "Wait. You let him stay the night?"

I glance at all three of my friends and they are gaping at me. "Yes."

"You must really like him," Emily finishes putting

creamer in her coffee. "I don't think you've let anyone stay the night. At least not since that one guy in college tried to cling to you."

That was when I stopped bringing people to my dorm room. It got weird and he wouldn't leave me alone for days after that. Xander seems different. He didn't act hurt or put out when I told him he needed to leave this morning. Though he did leave his number. Maybe that's just his way of putting the ball in my court and letting me decide if I want to make another move.

"He was nice, and we hit it off."

"How much younger than you is he?" Caroline narrows her eyes at me. I guess she has her reasons. I used to flirt with her brothers all the time once they were adults. At the time one of them was completely unavailable since he has a whole family, but the little one...I knew it got under her skin. So, I would do it for that reason alone.

"I don't know," I shrug and move to one of the shelves to lean against. "Early twenties? He was definitely old enough to be drinking, so you don't have to worry about that."

"Okay," Caroline sighs, "that's all I care about. I know they let eighteen and up in the bar, and I don't want you getting into trouble."

"I know how to watch out for myself, Care. It's how I made it through college."

I feel bad at the dig. It's not completely her fault she didn't go to college with us like we planned. She followed her heart even though it led to a horrific end.

"Point taken." She raises her hands in surrender.

Samantha grabs one of the stools and takes a seat. "So, are you going to see him again?"

I want to say no. Hell, I know I should, but I don't know if I will or not. I had fun with him last night. Even after we had sex, we were able to hang out and just live in the moment.

"I doubt it. Y'all, know I don't get serious with anyone. He did leave his number on a piece of one of my magazines before he left." I'm just grateful the piece didn't have any important information on it.

"So, he left the door open for a possibility." Emily takes a sip of her coffee.

"Yes, but...when exactly would I have time to date anyone. In case you haven't noticed, we have our hands full with the shop."

"I thought the same thing," Caroline smirks, "and now I have a whole boyfriend who adores me and David."

"That's you, though," I point out, "it's never something I've really looked for. You saw how my parents were growing up. That's not the type of life I want for myself."

"You realize that's not normal, right?" Samantha interjects. "It works for your parents, but that's not how every couple operates. Not that I'd know, or want to, from personal experience, but you get the drift."

"You can't exactly preach relationship advice to me when you don't do them either." I laugh. She would have to actually be nice to people to consider dating. The only people I've ever seen her let loose around is us, and that took a long time to happen when we were growing up.

"Why are you getting relationship advice?" Kai walks into the warehouse. Great. Now he's going to give me his input. Especially now that he's in his own little happy bubble of love. This is not what I need.

CHAPTER FOUR

xander

IT'S BEEN a week and Kate still hasn't called. Maybe I overstepped my bounds when I left my number. Or, I could have pushed for hers, but I don't think she would have appreciated that. She seemed to want me out of her apartment as soon as possible. She said it was work related and based on all the stuff on her coffee table, I believe her.

The sting doesn't go away, though. I thought we hit it off pretty well. I mean who else stays up drinking while making fun of infomercials. I know it's not something I've ever done before. There was a connection between us, and I don't think I'm the only one who felt it.

"Xander," Mom's voice echoes around the house, "you better be awake."

Ugh, this whole living situation sucks, and isn't at all how I imagined life after college would be. My entire plan banked on having job offers after I graduated, but no such luck. The places I have applied have passed me over for more experienced candidates. I'm right out of college, how am I supposed to gain experience if nobody will give me a chance.

"I'm up," I call out. I have been for *hours*, just like every morning for the past two weeks. The determination to find a job and get out of this house is strong. At this point, I'm not even paying attention to what the job is, I check to see if I meet the minimum requirements and fill out the form. Eventually one of these has to call me back, right?

There's a soft knock on my door before it cracks open and my mom pops her head inside. "Any luck?"

Honestly, I don't know if she just wants to help or wants me out. "Nope," I close my laptop, "do you think it's because I graduated in the winter instead of in the spring? Maybe that's why I didn't have any job offers."

"I doubt that," she walks in and sits on my bed. "You'll find something. It just might take more time than you thought."

"At least until then, I'm making a little something delivering pizzas. I just want something more stable."

"I know, kiddo," she pauses for a moment, "so, have you heard anything from that girl?"

This, ladies and gentlemen, is why I want out of this house. I love my mom, but between her constantly asking about the job search and asking about the woman I saw when I didn't come home that night, I'm going bonkers. There's no such thing as privacy with her. Which I can understand to an extent since it's her and dad's house, but I'm twenty-two. At some point she has to cut the cord, right? This is one of the few times I wish I had a sibling. Then they could share in the privacy invasion.

"No, Mom. I haven't heard from her." If I don't answer her, she'll keep harping on it. "I'm not sure if I ever will."

I hope I do, though. Anything serious is not something I'm ready for, but some fun when we both need to blow off steam doesn't feel like a horrible idea.

"Oh, okay. Well, I'm heading to the grocery store. Do you need anything, or want to come with me?"

As much as I want to scream absolutely not, I don't. It would only hurt her feelings. But I need to come up with an excuse. It's not like I can say work because she knows my shift at the pizza place doesn't start until this evening.

My phone pings, and I immediately check it. It's an email from one of the places I guess I applied to. "Actually, I think I might have a lead on a job. I'm going to call this guy back and see when he'd like me to interview."

"That's good news." she claps her hands, "text me if you think of anything you need."

"I will." She knows I'm not going to. I've been fairly independent for my entire life, and a part of me thinks that truly upsets her.

She stands from the bed and walks toward me, giving me a quick hug. "Good luck with your call. Who knows, it could be life changing."

I can only hope.

Lucky for me, the place had an interview open for today. I don't even know what the job is for, but it's worth checking out. After plugging in the address to my phone, I follow the map through town. Ideally, I wouldn't need the map. I mean, aside from college, I've lived here my whole life. The need to make sure I arrive at the correct address is stronger than relying on my memory.

It doesn't take long to get anywhere in this town. I park in front of the building and check my appearance before stepping out of my car. My uniform for the pizza place is in the backseat in case the interview runs long.

When I glance up at the sign, I see I've arrived at a flower shop. A spark of excitement zings across my body. Kate never said if her flower shop is in town or not. At least, not that I can remember. There's a possibility this isn't the one she owns with her friends. But...there's a chance it is. The fact the interview is at a florist has to have some sort of meaning, right?

I straighten my back, and head to the front door. I want to make the best impression possible on whoever is interviewing me on the off chance this is the shop Kate does in fact own.

A bell dings as I push the glass door open and step inside. The scent of flowers is overwhelming and something I'll have to get used to if I do get the job. Allergies aren't something I've ever dealt with, but my nose is starting to itch. Maybe it's because I haven't been around a lot of florals before.

"Hello?" I call out. There's nobody at the front counter, and I wonder if the man I talked to forgot about the interview. I've already forgotten his name because I was too excited about actually having an interview.

A tall guy walks out of a hallway behind the counter. "Hi, are you Xander?" He holds out his hand waiting for me to take it.

"Hi, yes. I'm Xander." I place my hand in his for a quick shake. "It's nice to meet you..."

I let the sentence hang in hopes he'll provide his name. "Kai."

"Sorry, I'm horrible with names."

"No problem." He gestures me to follow him. There's an open space between two of the glass counters, and I hurry through them after Kai. The hallway is narrow and short. He leads me to a small office to the right. "Take a seat."

There are two chairs, but only one directly in front of the desk so I choose that one to sit in. "Thank you for the opportunity to interview."

"No, thank you for being able to come in for it. We really need the help," he looks at a piece of paper on the desk. "Have you ever worked in a flower shop before?"

"I can't say that I have." I really hope this isn't something that will keep me from the job. "Right now, I deliver pizzas in the evenings. Work has been hard to come by considering I went to college."

"What's your degree in?"

"Business communications," I take a breath and let it out, "I haven't had much luck finding a job because they want experience, but nobody is willing to let me get that experience."

"I totally understand that," Kai laughs, "the business world is pretty cutthroat. All it takes is one person to give you a chance and doors will open."

"I hope so."

"You're actually overqualified for this job, but I do like that you have delivery experience. There are a few positions we need to fill. And, honestly, you were the first person to answer quickly, so you'll have first pick at what you want to do."

"What are the positions?" I feel like a dumbass for having to ask, but I don't want to admit that I was applying for jobs without looking over the details. That would probably make it seem like I'm unprofessional.

"We have a couple open to work the front counter during the day. We also need delivery drivers. The only caveat to that is we may need you some nights on the weekend. And then we have helping with the arrangements, but you don't have floral experience so that probably isn't the best job for you."

Depending on the pay, I may be able to do the deliveries and drop the pizza job for good. It's not a bad gig, but I do hate going home smelling like food. And it's almost impossible to get the smell out of my car. It's a wonder Kate didn't smell it when I took her home.

"What happens when there aren't deliveries to be made?"

He laughs, "It's cute you think it won't be that busy.

On the off chance there aren't any deliveries for a long amount of time, you'll help out here around the shop."

Wow. They must serve a wide base of clients to have that many deliveries. Weekends are busy with pizza deliveries, but we still have some lulls throughout the night. "And what do the people working the counter do?"

"Customer service, take orders, pull arrangements for people who come in to pick them up," he waves his hand around, "pretty much deal with people."

That doesn't sound terrible. Both are actually pretty doable from where I'm standing. Beggars can't be choosers and all that jazz. "What's the pay like?"

I know for a fact I didn't see that on there when I filled out the application. Some job listings had it and some didn't. It's the one piece of information I did look for.

"We'll start all employees out at fifteen an hour. Then it goes up from there based on job performance and quality of work. Right now, though, we really need a good driver."

That's more than I make delivering food, even when you add in the tips. The thought to wait a bit wiggles through my brain, but this is the best opportunity I've gotten. Well, the only one since I haven't heard from any of the other jobs.

"You've got yourself a driver." I open my arms wide.

"Great." Kai's shoulders sag in relief. It must have been a heavy weight on his shoulders. "I'll need to do a check on your driving record. I assume from your application you've never been in any accidents."

"No, sir."

He gasps, "I think that is the first time anyone has ever called me sir. I don't know if I like it."

"Sorry." He isn't that much older than me, but he's offering me a job, and I feel like it was the right word in the moment.

"No worries," he reaches into the desk and pulls out a few pieces of paper. "I just need you to fill these out and you have the job. The driving record shouldn't take more than a day or two. When can you start?"

"As soon as you need me. I just need to put in my notice at the other job."

"Sounds good," his phone rings and he hands me a pen, "I'll just be a minute."

Nodding, I take the pen and fill out the paper he needs for my driving record. I want to make sure he gets that going as soon as possible. It'll feel like a dream no longer smelling like pizza. The only thing I'll have to gauge is if I do in fact have allergies. I'll live through it, though. For now, it would be dumb to pass up this job.

I slide over that first form, and start on the rest. There aren't a ton of papers and I'm signing my name on the last one when he walks back into the office. "Woah, you got those done fast."

"Let's just say I'm eager to leave the pizza industry behind me."

"I don't blame you," he laughs, "I'll get started on this driving record ASAP. Are there any other questions you have for me?"

"Not really. It's not that hard to load a vehicle and

deliver. It's something I'm used to doing but the smell will be much better. You wouldn't believe some of the toppings folks want on their pizzas."

"Oh, I can imagine. I had this roommate that would add toppings for no other reason than to get a rise out of the rest of us when I was in college."

"Yeah, that's completely unnecessary."

"Agreed."

Laughter comes from somewhere down the hall interrupting our conversation. It's more than one person, and I could have sworn he said I was the first interview for the jobs in question.

"Looks like you'll get to meet your bosses."

"I thought you were my boss."

He stands and heads toward the door. "I am, but they are mine. I'm just the office manager."

Three women crowd into the small office, but only one of them catches my eye and my heart stops.

"Xander, this is Samantha, Emily, and my sister, Kate. They are the owners of Whoopsie Daisy." My stomach drops when he says Kate is his sister. This is going to be interesting.

Kate focuses in on me. "What are you doing here?"

"WAIT," my brother throws his hands up, "you know each other?"

Xander stares at me, unsure of what to do or say. Did he purposefully seek out the flower shop I own? I know I didn't give him a name when I told him what I do. All of this gives me those same feelings that one guy did in college. That guy also searched out where I worked.

"Really, Xander, why are you here?" I need to know if this is going to be a whole situation. All of this after I was thinking about calling him.

He points toward a stack of papers on the desk. "I, um, work here now."

Now that I'm studying him a bit more, maybe he didn't have ill intentions. His eyes are wide and it looks like he's paler than before. He must be as shocked as I am about his presence.

"Since when?"

"About five minutes ago," he stands, and straightens

his shirt, "I didn't know what the job was until I got here, and I swear I-I didn't know this was the shop you owned with your friends."

That makes sense, except…"What do you mean you didn't know what the job was. Did you not look at the applications you were filling out?"

Emily elbows me in the side. "Maybe y'all need some privacy."

Just great. In my shock at seeing Xander in our office, I completely forgot we're not alone. My friends, and brother, have their eyes glued to us. Emily is the only one nice enough to voice the faux pas. "Yeah, we probably do."

"Can someone fill me in on what's going on here?" Kai's voice booms in the silent room.

"Later," Samantha whispers as she punches him in the arm, "alright, shows over. We have orders we need to check over, and someone needs to be on the counter."

I'm surprised it wasn't Caroline that ushered everyone out. She's usually the person who takes charge. Leave it to my friends to puzzle out exactly who is in our office. I'm grateful they are letting me and him have this conversation in private.

Moving aside, I wait for them to file out of the office. Emily is the last person out and closes the door behind her. Thank goodness for small mercies.

"So, you really didn't know what type of job you were applying for?"

"Nope," he shakes his head. "I've been looking for

jobs for weeks now. At this point, I'm just looking for something better than delivering pizzas."

Oh, I didn't know that's what he was doing. Now I feel like a shitty person for not bothering to ask what he did when he opened up the conversation.

"You realize one of the jobs we have is for delivery drivers, right?"

"That's actually the job Kai, uh, your brother, just hired me to do. He let me pick which position I wanted but let me know that y'all really needed a driver. Besides, I'm good at that part," he picks at the hem of his shirt, "that is if I still have a job after your brother finds out we've been together."

"I'm sure he already knows." Honestly, I wouldn't be surprised if they are listening at the door. That's something they've done since we were kids. There's no such thing as privacy.

"Do you think he's going to fire me?" His voice wobbles, and I feel awful for him. Not because it's a fear he obviously has, but because there's a hint of desperation. It's the same one I felt when I graduated.

"Probably not." It's not a lie because we really need some people to ease the burden. "But do you think it's a good idea for you to work here? You know since we've, um, seen each other naked."

I'm trying my best to not raise my voice in case we really do have eavesdroppers. But I'm sure they've figured out the connection by now.

"Technically...the lights were off so I only saw shadows of your naked body with some strips of light from outside." He's not wrong. I kept the lights off for a reason. It takes some of the vulnerability out of the moment. If they are on, the person I'm with can see all my flaws. Under the cover of darkness, I can be in the moment without thinking too much. I also didn't know if I was going to see him again. The universe has to be screwing with me.

"That's beside the point." Why can't he see how this could be a problem. "We've had sex. It was supposed to be a one-night sort of thing. If you work here, we'll see each other on a daily basis."

He stands and leans against the desk. And damn if he doesn't look good while looking like he's at home in my office. "So, you didn't see that I left my number?" He takes a step toward me, "I know it was only supposed to be a one-night thing, but I like you. It's why I left my number."

Welp, I'm about to burst his bubble. "I did find your number." Hurt flashes across his face. I'm too freaked out right now to let him know I was considering calling him.

He takes a step back, putting distance between us. Ugh, I hate this. It's why I don't date anyone. I have my fun, and that's it. Being the person who has to hurt someone else's feelings isn't something I take joy in.

"You won't have to worry about me harassing you about a date if I'm working here," he lifts his wrist to check the time, "I really need this job. The one thing you can count on is me coming in and doing the work needed. Besides, if I'm making deliveries, how often am I really going to see you?"

Why does he keep making valid points? "Fine. I get what you're saying, and you're right." I take a deep breath and let it out, "the only time we'll see each other often is if we need you to deliver to a wedding venue, and when you're picking up orders."

"So, no more talk about me not working here?"

"No," I shove my hands in the pockets of my pants, "we're both adults. I think we can handle being around each other even though we've had naked fun times."

"Very adult way to put it," he laughs. He walks across the small space, and I wonder if maybe he didn't actually understand the conversation we just had. His arm brushes against mine as he reaches for the door handle. "I need to get to my job and put in my notice."

"Oh." Wait. Am I upset because he's doing exactly what he said he would. "Okay. I guess you'll be officially working here in the next couple of days?"

"Yep. Your brother has to check into a few things then I'll be here." He pulls open the door and heads out of the office.

Good. That gives me a few days to come to grips with whatever the hell it is I'm feeling. It's a mix of disappointment and excitement. What the hell is happening to me?

"You realize this has the potential to blow up in your face, right?" Samantha grunts as she spins the wreath she's working on around. It's for a baby shower this weekend, and she's not loving how she has the flowers placed.

"It's not like I told him to apply for a job here." I shrug.

"And you're sure you didn't say the name of the shop?" Emily asks. She's working on an order, but I have no idea what it is.

"Positive." They know damn well I keep things super casual. I don't give anyone any actual details about my life. Though I don't know why I offered up going to my apartment that night. It's not something I usually do. Another way for me to build a barrier. There's just something about Xander, and I can't quite put my finger on it.

"Kai seems to be taking it pretty well." Emily adds. Now she's grabbing flowers in various colors. None of them go together. What in the world is she putting together?

"Yeah, he is." Which is shocking to say the least. Especially after he figured out the connection between me and Xander. Normally it's something he would have given his two cents about. But he must have seen my reaction when I walked into the office after the interview a few days ago.

Speaking of, my brother walks into the back and looks over our tables. I have a couple of bouquets I'm working on. A guy is wanting to surprise his wife with flowers at work and at home to celebrate her promotion. It's a sweet gesture.

"What is that?" He points at the arrangement Emily

is working on. "I'm not a professional like the rest of you, but even I can tell it's a mess."

Emily shrugs and continues adding flowers to the vase. "It's what the client wanted. Apparently, all of these are the favorite colors of the girl he's trying to impress. He was waiting by the front door when I got here this morning."

"That's...odd." Kai runs a hand through his hair.

"Not really," another flower goes in the vase, "he didn't want to be late for school so I took his order before we technically opened."

Ah, now it makes sense. "Are we supposed to deliver those to the high school?"

"No," she shakes her head, "he doesn't want to embarrass her. He asked me to deliver them to her house this afternoon."

"More like he doesn't want to get rejected in front of his classmates," Kai smirks, "I remember that feeling all too well."

"Like you ever got rejected by a girl," Samantha laughs and rolls her eyes, "from what I remember, you had girls waiting for a chance to go out with you."

"And we see how that turned out," my brother shakes his head, "not that it matters anymore since I have an actual girlfriend." He studies the vase of mismatched flowers. "Come to think of it, I should probably get her some flowers."

"You better learn how to arrange your own bouquet," Samantha says, "none of us have time to add another job to our plates right this second."

"I never said it was for today. Maybe next week when she has a day off."

"Add it to the calendar," I point toward the huge whiteboard that covers the wall above the coffee maker.

"We're supposed to be going digital," he mumbles under his breath as he moves toward the board. He grabs a dry erase pen and opens it. "Where exactly do I add it? It looks like next week is completely booked up."

"As long as it's not a huge arrangement, I can squeeze it in." Seeing my brother happy, fills me with joy. He dated someone when he lived away from home, but it didn't end well. Then he got into an argument with his boss and left his job. Now he's helping us. "Put it wherever."

He scribbles his arrangement on the calendar. "I'll also add this to the group calendar. If we're going to make this all work, y'all need to start using it."

"It's hard to break habits," Emily grins. "That board has been with us since the beginning. It's nostalgic."

"Well, if we're going to keep up with the growth, some things have to be moved to the digital realm." He shakes his head and walks back toward the office. "Oh, now I remember what I came in here to tell you. Xander's driving record came back. It's good. Do you want to contact him?"

"Isn't that your job?" I argue.

"Yes, but I have another person coming in for an interview in a few minutes before I handle whatever deliveries you have," he stops in the hallway, "which would you rather me do?"

"Fine I'll do it." I could mention that he would have had time if he didn't comment on Emily's order or realize he needs to get his girlfriend flowers.

I add the last bits of greenery to the vase I have before pulling out my phone. I've had his number saved since I found it on my coffee table. The urge to call him over the past week has been strong, but I've held back. Now, I don't have a choice. Now do I text or call him. My thumb hovers over his name.

xander

MY PHONE RINGS on the nightstand. I don't have to worry about it being about a job interview since I technically have one. Instead of answering it, I let it go to voicemail. Right now, I'm looking for apartments online. Being able to move right away isn't realistic, but I want to at least get an idea of how much I need to save.

In college I had roommates so we split the rent. Now, though, it'll just be me. Unless, of course, I can't afford it on my own. Then I'll be looking for roommates. Staying with my parents is not how I want to live long term. Especially if I meet someone special.

My finger hovers over the icon to bookmark the current page. The apartment complex isn't too far from where Kate stays, but it's closer to the shop. More importantly, it's within my budget. I'm not sure if that's a good thing or not.

The phone rings again, and I jump, almost falling out of my chair. Turning toward my bed, I rush to the phone.

It has to be important if whoever it is calling back-to-back. The number isn't one I recognize. I swipe to answer. "Hello?"

"Xander?" I know that voice anywhere. "It's Kate."

"Hey, what's up?" There are only two ways she could have gotten my number. From the slip of paper, I left it on, or my paperwork.

"I was just letting you know your driving record came back."

"Okay..."

"Oh, it's clean. You can start working here as soon as possible." The words come out in a rush. Is it bad that I feel a small sense of joy that I make her nervous after our conversation in the office? Probably.

"That's actually really good. Tonight is my last night delivering pizzas." Apparently, they didn't want me working longer than necessary. It's fine by me, at least I gave my notice like a responsible employee. "I can start tomorrow."

"That would be great."

Kate delivering the news is odd. "I thought Kai was going to call?"

I can hear the sigh over the phone. "He was supposed to, but he had another interview to get to."

Well, so much for me hoping she was giving me the update so she could talk to me. "What time do I need to get there?"

"Why don't we shoot for eight? It'll give us a chance to go over how the flowers needs to be loaded and all that.

"I'll be there." For most people this would be weird. But I'll put whatever feelings I have aside for a better job. At least…for now.

"See you in the morning." She doesn't wait for me to respond and hangs up. Huh. I guess I'll see how she reacts to me in the morning. All I know is I'm not showing up empty handed.

I slam my hand against my phone as soon as the beeping starts. Sleeping in isn't something I typically do, but this is the first time I've *had* to be up in a long time. Rubbing my hands down my face, I kick my comforter aside. I don't have to be at the shop for two hours, but I want to make the best first impression and have time to get donuts. Showing up with food is never a bad idea, and based on Kate's reaction after the night we spent together…I don't think she remembers to eat breakfast for work.

Is it an overstep? Maybe. Keeping things professional is something I fully intend to do. Bringing donuts for the office is a good thing for everyone. Now I need to figure out what to wear. Kai was in jeans and nice shirt when I interviewed with him. It's probably the safest route to go on the first day. I have no idea if they have uniform shirts for drivers. None of them had anything specific to Whoopsie Daisy.

Or…maybe I'm overthinking things. Even though I want to impress Kate, I also want to keep this job. It could be long term, or short term, that's yet to find out. But for now, I need the money. I need to feel like I control my future in some aspect, and this is the first step in doing that.

It only takes me a few minutes to pull clothes out of my closet. I moved all of my nice garments to the front a couple of weeks ago in case I had an interview. Also, I think I need new clothes. Most of them are from college and I didn't exactly dress to impress during the lectures. Most of the time it was whatever I rolled out of bed in. I guess I know what I will be doing with my first check after I see what they want me to wear.

Shockingly my mom is awake when I head downstairs. Eggs are scrambling in a skillet while she adds bacon to a frying pan. "What's the occasion?"

She only cooks breakfast for dinner, or on the weekends and when we have family in town. "I wanted to make sure you had a decent meal before you left for work."

That's actually pretty sweet of her. Not that she's a horrible mom or anything. My biggest issue with living at home is her tendency to be overbearing. She has to butt into my life whenever she thinks it's necessary, which is all the time.

"You didn't have to do that."

"It's fine, Xan, I want to," she flips a piece of bacon, "I know you won't always be living here, and I want to soak in these moments."

The sadness over my moving out stabs me in the gut. I should probably cut her some slack. I know it can't be easy. She's provided for me all these years, aside from when I was away at college, and it has to be weird knowing her only child doesn't really need her the way I used to.

I give her a quick hug because I don't want to be popped with bacon grease, and soft peck on top of her head. "Thanks, Mom."

It kind of ruins the appetite for donuts, but it's fine. This makes Mom happy, and I don't want to pull away from that. I pull out the plates from the cabinet and set them on the table. Footsteps thumb on the stairs and I pull out another plate.

"It smells delicious in here." Dad walks into the kitchen and straight toward Mom. He pulls her to him and kisses her like they are still in the newlywed stage instead of being married for thirty years. It's sweet and horrifying at the same time.

"Ugh, gross," I cover my face with my hands, "can y'all not do that in front of me?"

"Not going to happen," Dad grins as he pulls away from her. "You act like we haven't done this every day for your entire life."

"Yeah, but not first thing in the morning."

Mom turns off the burners on the stove and moves the pans to the back. "Xander, I hope you find someone that makes you want to make out with them every day for the rest of your lives."

"Please make it stop."

Dad's laugh echoes around the room. I'm almost certain they do this just get a rise out of me. Don't get me wrong, there's nothing wrong with a little PDA, but that doesn't mean I want to see it.

"So, today's your first day at the new job?" Dad takes a plate and loads it up with food.

"Yep," I follow after him, "it's pretty much the same thing I was doing delivering pizzas, only this time it's flowers."

"As long as you're happy doing it, I don't care what you do." Dad claps a hand on my shoulder before taking a seat at the table.

"We'll see. I mean how hard can it be?" I sit down and take a bite of food. "I know they said there will also be weekends when I work because they do the flowers for a lot of weddings. But the pay is better so I'm not complaining. And I think Kate and her friends will be easy to work with. They take a lot of pride in their business."

"Wait," Mom says as she sits, "isn't Kate the name of that girl you were with the other night?"

Ugh, I knew it was a mistake when I mentioned her name. "Yes," I draw out.

Dad sets his fork down and studies me. "I won't tell you what to do, but be careful when mixing business with personal relationships. It can go downhill pretty quickly."

"I, uh, don't think that will be a problem. She made it pretty clear we won't be seeing each other." Another bite to buy myself some time, "as much as I wish it were otherwise, I want this job. And I didn't know she owned the shop until after I signed the employee paperwork."

"Well," Mom breathes a sigh of relief, "that makes me feel better."

I finish off my food and scoot my chair back. "I need to finish getting ready. Leave the dishes, I'll get them done before I head out."

I don't give either of them a chance to respond before I hurry back up the stairs. As much as I appreciate their words, I don't really need them freaking me out more than I already am. Overthinking has become my super power.

There's a line of people behind me at the donut shop. The lady at the front counter is patient, and that's more than I can say about those behind me. Most of them look like teens trying to get their breakfast on the way to school, and I feel bad for holding them up.

But I have no clue what everyone likes, or if they have any food allergies. The last thing I want to do is make someone go to the emergency room because they ate something I brought. I guess it's best to keep it simple.

"Can I get a dozen donuts, half glazed and half chocolate. A dozen pigs, and six bottles of orange juice?"

"Sure thing." She gives me the total and I pay. It's a good thing tips were good over my last few days at the last job. "Can you stand right over there while they get your order together?"

"Absolutely." Such a nice way to tell me to get out of the way so they can get the line down. I get why it's packed. This is the best donut shop in town. Although it's kind of funny there are two donut shops in a town this small. I don't even know how the other one stays in business, but I don't go to that side of town very often.

Within a few minutes my order is brought out and I struggle to get the door open. Maybe I'm doing too much, but I don't care. At least everyone will start the day off with something to eat. I set the boxes and bag on top of my car, hoping the wind doesn't knock them off, before unlocking and putting them in the passenger seat.

The flower shop is two streets over, and it doesn't take me long to get there. Unsure of where to park, I pull into the same spot I had when I came in for my interview. I'm early and the lights are still off inside the shop, but I see Kai lingering by the front door.

Before I'm all the way out of the car, he cracks the door open. "Go down the alley and pull around back. We have parking there for employees."

"You got it." I watch him close and lock the door before turning away. I guess he was waiting for me. Though it would have been nice to know where I park from the beginning, I know now.

Now that I'm safely parked behind the shop, I notice there aren't very many cars. There should be at least five, but aside from mine there are only three, plus the two delivery vans. I grab the boxes and bag before opening my door and stepping out.

Kai is at the door holding it open. "This will give you brownie points," he points toward the boxes in my hand, "just please don't say anything if you're using it as a way to get into my sister's pants. That's more information than I want to have."

He seems to be pretty chill about knowing Kate and I saw each other. It was just once, but I don't think that typically matters when it comes to siblings. Though, I wouldn't know since it's just me. "Where is everyone?"

"The only one missing is my sister." He leads me to a table in the middle of the room. I didn't get to see this space the other day. It's like a mini warehouse with shelves of vases, wire wreaths, and flowers. Each section properly labeled. "She started walking to work, like she usually does, but said it was too windy and went back for her car."

"Why does she walk?" I know her apartment isn't too far from here, but I still wouldn't walk it every day.

"I don't know. She said it helps her think and keeps her moving." That makes sense.

"Well, hopefully everyone is hungry." I set the boxes on the table. "I also brought orange juice. I wasn't sure what everyone liked."

"They usually live off of coffee." Kai points to the coffee maker in the corner. "I honestly don't see how any of them get actual sleep with the amounts of caffeine they take in every day, but to each their own. I'll go let the ladies know there's food."

He walks toward the hallway and disappears into the office. I take a moment to study the room around me. Other than the van, it looks like this is where I'll spend most of my time. I move toward the shelves, glancing over the labels and get a feel for where everything is.

There's another shelf that's mostly empty with a label that says deliveries. It's close to the door and where I assume I'll be pulling orders.

I take a step to go down one of the aisles, but the door opens with a gust of wind and Kate walks in. Her hair is whipping in the wind behind her and she looks ethereal. Her eyes widen when she sees me and I don't know if it's because I'm actually here or if she's surprised I showed up early.

Pointing toward the table in the middle of the room, I take a step toward her instead of further into the warehouse area. "I brought donuts."

Why is that the first thing that pops out of my mouth. I'm a freaking idiot.

XANDER in the middle of the warehouse isn't what I expect to see as soon as I open the door. I'm fifteen minutes early, which is a miracle in itself. But that's only because I usually walk to work. I am a little shocked to see that he was looking at the shelves. I don't think even Kai knows where everything is, and he's been working with us for a few months. Maybe we really can work together with no hard feelings.

I follow his finger as he points to the work table. There are in fact boxes of donuts sitting on the edge. We really need to do something about getting a break area. "Thank you." I step further inside the warehouse and take off my jacket. The door slams shut behind me, and I jump. "You didn't have to do that."

"I know, but the other morning you ran out in a rush, and I have a feeling you don't stop to eat breakfast most mornings."

"So, you did it for me?" This will be more difficult

than I thought. I can't have him coming in here being all thoughtful and adorable doing nice things for me. It'll make it that much harder to keep everything on a professional level. Even after our exchange after his interview earlier this week, I haven't been able to stop thinking about him. Hell, I haven't even gone out, aside from last night when we had our girls' night. All of the things I do on a normal basis have flown out the window.

He takes a step back. "N-no. It wasn't just for you," he looks around, "I brought it for everyone. I even grabbed some orange juice just in case, but Kai informed me when I got here that y'all drink coffee like its water."

I feel slightly better at the admission. At least it wasn't just for me. That would have been weird. We also live off of donuts here. At this point, I feel like we should have an order ready every morning.

"It's fine." My smile is tight. The need to give off neutral feelings is high. I have to go the extra mile to control my face expressions. Glancing around the warehouse, I don't see anyone else. "Where is everyone?"

"Kai went to get them a few minutes ago, but they haven't come out of the office yet." Xander points at the shelves. "I was just looking over everything so I know where things are."

"That's actually pretty awesome." I take a few steps into the room and throw my jacket on an empty chair. "Most of what you'll need will be on this shelf over here. But when you aren't making deliveries, it's good to know where everything is."

I walk along the line of shelves, closer to Xander.

"Pretty much everything in this area stays the same. They are the basic flowers that most people want and we've learned how many to keep in stock on a daily basis."

"That means people in Asheville order flowers every day." He's in awe at the sheer number of blooms sticking out of buckets.

I move toward the wall and pull the blinds open. It's not sunny, but it helps to have as much light as possible in here. I'm doing everything I can to avoid the lamps if I can help it. "We don't just service Asheville. At least, not anymore. We have deliveries in the surrounding cities."

"What made y'all become popular all of a sudden?" He's genuinely curious. Not that I blame him. Our rise to the top in our county wasn't anything we controlled.

"So, you know the band Crooked Halo?"

"You know them?" The pitch of his voice goes up an octave. I take it he's a fan.

"We didn't until a couple of months ago." I shake my head at the whirlwind our business has become. "Their business manager is getting married and his fiancée is the cousin of the person who creates the buzz for Out of the Ashes. She only wanted to use us for the floral arrangements and decor."

"I don't see how that has anything to do with y'all."

"Their business manager, Spencer, and his fiancée, Tiffany, are beloved by the Crooked Halo fans. I think they are kept up with as much as the band." Honestly, it's pretty impressive the fanfare they get. "As soon as the fan in this area realized that, they've been booking us for special events, deliveries, and anything else they need. Which I'm not upset about. It's just...a lot."

He's nodding as I explain the situation. "That actually makes a lot of sense. Fandoms can go a little bananas. But it's great they want to support a small business. It's better than them using the big box names for their needs. And it helps y'all become the go-to place for flowers. I guess this is why y'all need to hire people as soon as possible."

"You'd be correct," I point at him, "our calendar is filling up. Kai still helps with deliveries but it's not something he loves to do. He'd much rather be in the shop and managing people."

"I get that feeling." That's not what I expected him to say.

"Why did you want to work here?"

He takes a moment to think it over. "Honestly, I needed a better paying job. Living with the folks isn't something I want to do for much longer. And this was the first opportunity that came up."

"If you get a better offer from someone, I want you to take it."

He whips his head back like I've physically slapped him. "Why? I haven't even started my first day here?"

"Because I know if you have a degree, you're way overqualified for this shop. Just like my brother is," I shake my head and turn toward the hallway. "He's staying on here by choice. I don't want our shop to be the reason you stay at a job that doesn't challenge you."

I don't notice him move, but within seconds his

hand covers my shoulder. Stopping in my tracks, I look over my shoulder. "How about you let me decide what is challenging? I'm here to do a job and do it well. Right now, this is the best offer I've had. But I need you to stop second guessing me and let me do what I need to."

"Um, okay." There's nothing else I can say to that. Although the way he is making his point known without letting me push him over is kind of a turn on. Something I absolutely do not need right now. "I'm gonna see where everyone else is."

As soon as the words are out of my mouth, my friends and brother emerge from the office. Kai looks frustrated, but my friends...they are smiling. What in the world are they up to? Whatever it is, my brother is not on board.

***

Emily takes the reins and shows Xander where everything is in the warehouse. Caroline is busy getting a few bouquets done that need to go out this afternoon. Which leaves me and Samantha working the front counter. Honestly, I don't know if it takes two of us, but we might as well.

Our phones keep pinging with updates from Kai about wedding appointments. He made us all subscribe to the calendar for Whoopsie Daisy that he created. Each appointment has a list of information in the notes section. We really were underutilizing him when he was making deliveries. Handling the business side of things seems to be where he thrives.

"Please tell me these pings will end when we close the shop for the day," Samantha groans as another one goes off. "The last thing I want is to be in the middle of watching something and my phone going off."

"Stop being such a grump. At least we have business," I bump my shoulder into hers, "just think about all those years we didn't know how we were going to stay open. This is a good problem to have."

"True," she concedes, "but we're also about to hit the Valentine's Day rush. If we don't get a few more employees in here quickly, we won't be able to keep up. They'll go online and order from one of those places that overcharges."

"Naw," I wave my hand at her, "you know this town is all about community. They'll patiently wait if they have to."

"It's not them I'm worried about," Samantha grunts, "I'm going to see if Caroline needs any help with the arrangements. I saw another order come in through the email."

"Okay." She leaves me to my thoughts and right now that's a scary place to be. Xander flits through them, and I need those to stop. I was grateful when Emily offered to show him around. Being anywhere near him is not good for my sanity. Who knew I could feel any sort of connection to someone I barely know.

The bell above the door jingles as it opens. A gush of

air follows Caroline's brother into the shop. "Hey, Reaf, what can I do for you today?"

"Is it too early to order something for Valentine's Day?" He glances around the room seeing what flowers we have on display. Some of them need to be sold today, or we'll need to toss them.

"Not at all." I pull out a pen and the notepad we use to take orders. A part of me wonders if that is something else my brother is going to upgrade. It probably needs it. "The earlier the better."

"Good," he taps his fingers against the glass counter-top. "I need two bouquets. But I don't know what to get. Roses seem overdone and they aren't Tonya's favorite."

"Are both of them for her?"

"No," he laughs, "one is for Layla's birthday."

"That is sweet. She'll be excited to get her own flowers."

"Yeah, that's what I'm hoping," he looks around the room again, hoping something pops out at him, "any suggestions?"

"We can do some fun-colored chrysanthemums for Layla." I think about the little girl in question. She's definitely not one for muted colors. She likes bold and loud. "Let me think about what else to add in. The perk of coming to us is we know her, so maybe we can all add a little something from each of us."

"That would be amazing, and I know she'll love it." He taps on the counter again. "Now, what about Tonya?"

"No matter what we decide, I do think some roses

will be okay. But I think a more subtle color scheme. Let me see what we have on order and I can let you know."

The grin Reaf has on his face is what makes having this shop worth it. "Sounds awesome," he glances at his watch, "I better get back to the shop. Johnny was freaking out about a bunch of oil changes showing up out of nowhere."

"I'll give you a call in a couple of hours once I've talked with the girls."

"Let me know how much I owe and I'll stop by after work." He turns and walks out the door.

"I think I went to school with his brother." I jump at the sound of Xander's voice.

"How long have you been there?" I glance toward the hallway.

"Not long," he gestures toward Reaf's retreating figure on the sidewalk. "Caroline's his sister, right?"

"Yep." At least the focus isn't on me. This I can handle. "You probably went to school with Bryce, he's the youngest."

"Yeah, he played football. I didn't hang out with him, but I knew who he was."

"That's cool." I don't know what else to say to that. "Did Emily get you settled?"

"I know where everything is," he points behind him, "there are a few deliveries that need to be taken out, but Emily said I need someone to ride with me today."

"Yeah, she likes to control what situations she can." I rip the piece of paper off the notepad and stick it in my pocket. "I'll grab Kai and tell him he needs to ride with you."

We walk down the hallway and the door to the office is halfway open. My brother is on the phone, and it sounds like he's setting up an interview. Well crap, I guess he's out since he's fielding calls.

"I don't think he'll be able to," Xander mimics my thoughts, "maybe one of the others?"

"Maybe." Though I'm not holding out much hope. I know Caroline has to leave in a bit for something with her son, which leaves Sam or Emily.

Both of them are finishing up some arrangements when we walk into the warehouse. "Can one of y'all drive around with Xander for these deliveries?"

Samantha shakes her head. "No, I have an appointment with bride. She wants to know every kind of flower we offer. I have a feeling I'm not going to like this one." I swear she better fix her mood before she gets to the appointment.

"I was going to handle the front counter. I need to leave when the shop closes. My parents are requesting a mandatory dinner." Emily says.

"Mandatory doesn't sound like a request," Xander laughs.

"You haven't had the pleasure of meeting my parents," Emily grins, "I guess that leaves you. Kai doesn't have any appointments for you until tomorrow."

Damn it. That's what I was afraid of. I'll be alone with Xander in a van for a few hours. Maybe I'll get lucky and he won't talk much. "I guess you're stuck with me."

CHAPTER EIGHT

xander

I'M NOT sure if I should be offended or not. Kate was doing everything in her power to keep from riding with me. Secretly, though, I'm excited it's her. I mean, I would have been fine with anyone, but this gives me time alone with her. Who knows...maybe we'll even get to know each other a little better. At least, enough to where she isn't freaking out every time we're alone together.

"Where do we keep the van keys?" My eyes bounce around the walls to see if there is some sort of hook holding them.

"Crap. They're in the office," Kate holds up a finger, "I'll be right back."

"Y'all should probably put something out here to hold them so the drivers aren't constantly going to the office."

"Probably," Samantha shrugs, "we'll get around to it. It's not like it's ever been more than us."

Emily motions for me to come closer to them at the

work station. A few donuts are still in the box in the middle. It's a wonder there aren't any flower pieces inside it.

"A few tips. Don't come off too forward. Kate is used to being the one in charge. Also, any sort of serious relationship sends her running for the hills. She has this thing about them because of her parents. Don't ask, she'll tell you when and if she's ready."

"I'm not sure I know what you're talking about." Am I that easy to read?

"I know you didn't expect her to be your boss, but this is one of those time fate is working in your favor. Don't screw it up." Emily glances toward the hall to make sure Kate isn't coming. "Let her lead the way. She'll come around."

"How do you know? She seems pretty set against it."

"Because we can all see the way she looks at you when she thinks nobody is paying attention." Samantha adds before picking up one of the donuts. She opens her mouth to take a bite but stops. "Just don't screw her over. She's precious with her heart and only lets those she trusts in."

"Got them," Kate calls from warehouse entrance, "do you have the delivery orders?"

Emily hands me a stack of papers. "They're right here."

"Thanks, Em." Kate smiles. It's real and genuine. The same one she gave while we were watching infomercials and mocking them. I've missed that in the times we've seen each other since then.

"You ready to go?" I gesture toward the door.

"Yep." She walks out in front of me. Emily gives me a thumbs up before I follow after Kate.

She's already sitting in the passenger seat when I make it to the van. My fingers are gripped around the papers as I open the door with my free hand. This wind is ridiculous, and I hope it stops soon. "Samantha loaded the van while I was getting you. It doesn't look like there are a lot of deliveries."

"Where are they at?"

I start the van before I leaf through the papers. "It looks like five of them are in Dallas, and there's a few here in Asheville. Where should we start?"

"Asheville," she nods toward the exit, "it's best to get these out of the way before we hit traffic."

"Shouldn't that be the other way around to avoid traffic?" None of these are time sensitive. They just need to be delivered today.

"Nope." She shakes her head and holds out her hand for the orders. "I like to start with our locals. They've kept us in business all these years so they get top priority."

"Makes sense." I glance over them one more time before handing them to her. "I'll start with the ones furthest from the highway and work our way toward it."

"Now you're thinking like us." She gives me a wide, real smile. "It's best to do it that way so we don't have to double back. Make sure to note the time on the page here." She points at a line on the paper. "Then we note the times as we go along. It gives us an idea of how long we spend at each location."

"Alright." I grab a pen from the cupholder and make a note of the time. "Let's do this."

***

"You got that done in record time." Kate smiles as we get back on the highway. Eight stops in a few hours isn't too shabby. "Keep this up and Kai might get jealous you've outdone him."

"Delivering pizzas gives a sense of urgency." I check my blind spot before getting in the next lane. "People are not happy if they don't get their pizzas quickly. It turns into this whole thing. I've learned to be quick."

"I can appreciate that." A quick glance at her and she's pulling out her phone. I don't let my eyes linger much longer than a second. Traffic is heavy and the last thing I want to do on my first day is get in a wreck.

"It looks like there's a lot of brake lights up ahead," I nod to show my point. "Is there anything on the map?"

"Give me just a second," her fingers tap against the screen and she groans, "it looks like the backup is for a few miles. I'd say to go around, but we missed our last chance at an exit before the backup begins."

"Maybe it won't take too long to get through it."

"Doubtful, but I'm crossing my fingers."

We finally come up on the traffic and everyone is at a standstill. Whatever happened, it must be bad. "Are you sure there aren't any other exits to take?"

I'm not trying to speed up my time with her, but I also don't want to be stuck in this. It's not my driving I'm worried about. Everyone else makes me nervous, especially with folks on their phones when they shouldn't be. Too many people I know have gotten into accidents for that reason alone.

"There's one I didn't see before, but it's just as backed up as the highway." She runs a hand through her hair, working out the tangles at the end. "And it looks like it would take us a much longer way around."

"Damn," I mutter, "well, once we get past this, we can always pick up something to eat. I'm sure everyone at the shop will be gone by the time we get there."

"Probably. We close in thirty minutes." She doesn't address my other suggestion. Emily was right, I really shouldn't push things. "At least we got all of our deliveries done. That's the important part."

"Will you need to ride with me tomorrow, too?" Part of the question is curiosity because I want to spend more time with her away from everyone else. The other is so I know what to expect.

"I don't think so." She grabs two bottles of water from her bag and hands one to me. "You seemed to manage it just fine today. I think you're a great addition to our team."

"And you were worried I wouldn't be able to do my job." I inch the van up since we've moved all of two feet. "I told you, I'm a good delivery driver."

"You know good and well, that wasn't why I was concerned."

"I know, but it doesn't negate the fact I'm good at what I do." In more ways than one. The words don't have to be said, they are hanging in the air. She must think the same thing because her cheeks turn pink.

"Oh, it looks like traffic is moving." She points ahead of us, changing the subject effectively.

"I don't know that going five miles per hour is moving, but at least there's motion."

"That's kind of the definition of moving." I can feel her roll her eyes.

"You're right." We've been sitting in traffic for almost an hour. We aren't getting up to normal speeds but at least it's forward progress. "When do you typically have busy days? Today felt kind of slow with deliveries."

"We'll have a higher volume tomorrow and over the weekend." She glances at her phone again. "Most people send flowers on Fridays and then we have weddings we have to get deliveries to on the weekends. We try to take Sunday off, but there's the occasional bride who has a wedding on that day because venue prices are slightly less expensive."

"Do we have any of those this weekend?" I accepted that I'd have to work weekends.

"We have a wedding Saturday evening we have to deliver. But if you already have plans you don't have to be there. It is your first few days after all," she takes a sip of her water, "I'm also sure Kai didn't mention anything about this weekend."

"He didn't," I agree, "but I can drive one of the vans. I don't have anything else going on."

The most I planned on doing was playing video games or watching a movie. Going to the bar crossed my mind, but I wasn't sure how exhausted I'd be after this week.

"That's great. Kai will be happy to hear it." Her thumbs move over her phone. The soft taps filling the silence. "His girlfriend miraculously got the night off and he was hoping to take her out."

"Where does his girlfriend work?"

"Out of the Ashes. She's one of the chefs."

Does everyone date someone from the bar? "I didn't realize how interconnected everyone got when I left for college."

"That's mostly Stella's magic." Her voice is a soft laugh. "I wouldn't be surprised if she starts doing event planning. She's the reason Out of the Ashes is the success it is now."

"Sounds like it. This town could use a little shaking up in terms of people coming out. I'm glad it seems to be working for everyone."

"Yeah, it really has turned into a closeknit community. Even more than it used to be."

"Good." The traffic picks up speed and I'm grateful we can head home. "Looks like we might make it back before it's too late."

Kate stares out the window. "I wonder what the holdup was. I don't see anything."

"It was probably cleaned up while we were sitting way back there. That would explain why we were sitting still for so long."

"Probably."

The rest of the ride back to Asheville is silent. She's working on her phone. Thank God the ping noises stopped. I'm not sure how she deals with that. It would drive me up the wall.

All the cars, except ours, are gone when we pull into the back parking lot. Kate pulls out a set of keys from her bag as she opens the van door. I grab the delivery slips before stepping out. It takes her a minute to get the door unlocked. But as soon as it's open, I follow her inside.

"Where do you want me to put these?" I hold the papers in the air.

She turns to see what I'm doing. "In the office is fine." She checks over a large whiteboard they have on the wall by the coffee pot. I didn't even notice it before. "I need to see if they've left any notes for in the morning."

"Don't y'all have everything on a digital calendar now?"

"It's going to take some time for us to get used to that system. It's brand new, and none of us are ready to give up the white board."

To each their own, I guess. "I'll be right back."

The hallway to the office is dark. The light from the warehouse doesn't make it through here, and I don't know where the switch is to turn it on. Pulling my phone out of my pocket, I turn on the flashlight. The office door is open and the desk is cleared of any papers. I have a feeling Kai isn't going to be happy with papers magically appearing on it. I add the van key before I forget it in my pocket.

Once that's done, I head back toward the warehouse. Kate is still at the white board. She's copying notes from the order she took before the deliveries. I think it's sweet they are personalizing the bouquets that were requested. I guess it's a perk of being part of the family. I don't know all the details, but I'm pretty sure they all grew up together.

"Do you need anything else?"

She doesn't turn around. "Can you make sure there's nothing in the back of the van and lock it up?"

"Absolutely." The air is colder as I push open the back door. The can is right outside and I pull open the door on the back. There are a few stems that fell off the flowers and I grab those before checking the lock. Then I head to the front doors and lock them by hand.

Hurrying back inside, I toss the stems in the trash. "Everything is locked up."

"Thanks." She sets the paper on the counter and heads toward the door. Grabbing the jacket she forgot earlier, she opens the back door. "You can head out if you want. I'm just going to set the alarm and head home."

Nodding, I walk out the door. I'm not leaving until I know she's safely in her car. As much as I would love to grab dinner with her. I feel like that's not going to happen.

It takes a few minutes before she finally walks out the door. "Oh, you're still here."

"I didn't mean to scare you." I shove my hands in my pockets. Note to future self, bring a jacket. "I wanted to make sure you got out okay."

"Um, thanks." She looks everywhere but at me.

"Want to grab some food?"

She doesn't answer for a few seconds, and I think she might say yes. "It's actually getting pretty late. I think I'm going to call it a night and head home."

"Okay." I had to shoot my shot.

"Maybe some other time, though." I feel like she's tossing me a bone. Not that I blame her. I did tell her I could keep it professional. I'm failing epically in the respect.

"Sure. Sounds good." I move to my car and open the door. "Night, Kate."

"Goodnight, Xander," she waves at me, "you did great for your first day."

I wait until she gets in her car and drives off before I start mine. Working with Kate is going to be a lot harder than I thought.

THE SHOP IS full of noise since we've hired more people. I don't know what magic Kai has worked, but we filled every position we needed. We have two people who rotate working the counter and another driver that works along with Xander. They draw straws for who is going to take the route for Dallas. It's funny watching them. Some days they even do rock, paper, scissors.

I had reservations about Xander working here, but he fits in with the team really well. More than I thought he would. Even Kai grabs lunch with him if they are here at the same time. I don't know why it matters if my brother can get along with him. It's not like we're dating or anything. The stolen glances when we think the other isn't looking is pretty telling, though. Weeks have passed and we're in our busiest season of the year.

"Kate," Caroline calls from across the warehouse, "where are the chrysanthemums? We need to get this order together for my brother."

"They aren't back there?" I'm working on Tonya's arrangement. It's a mixture of daisies, roses, and a couple of wildflowers. I wanted to keep it simple for her since that's the vibe she gives.

"If they were do you think I'd be asking?" She's never this short with us and I wonder if David's dad is giving them problems. He cleaned up his act for a while, but I know he still likes to throw a wrench in their lives when he can. I wish he'd just let her and Carlos be happy.

"I've got it, Kate," Xander rushes by me, "the delivery came in before you got here. I didn't have time to put them where they belong."

"Thanks, Xan." Woah, when I did start shortening his name. That's something for close friends or relationships. "But hurry, we've got deliveries stacking up."

"You got it."

I don't think he was fully prepared for the chaos Valentine's Day brings. Everyone tries to outdo previous years bouquets. Honestly, it's a little sad that most of these people only show how much they *love* each other one day a year.

I glance at the monitor Kai set up on the counter in front of the white board. Last minute orders are flying in. There's no way we're going to get all these out before the end of the day. Turning around, I make my way to the office.

Kai is sitting behind the desk updating the romance playlist he has playing through all the speakers. It's a wide range, I'll give him that. "You're going to be mad at me."

"Why?" He glances up from the screen.

"We need help with deliveries."

"Can't we just cut off taking orders?" It's a viable option, but not one I'm keen on taking.

"Nope," I shake my head, "you can take my car if you want to keep the miles off yours. Paula and Winston have the counter covered. But I need to help put together orders."

"Fine." He grumbles. After pressing a few buttons, he stands. "We really need to think about getting a third van and driver. Maybe not all the time, but definitely for the busy seasons."

"You're right," I clap my hands together, "but that will have to wait until our next meeting. Right now, we need to get these orders out the door."

"Have Xander and Robert already chosen their routes?" He knows about the way they choose.

"Yes. Xander has all the deliveries in Asheville, and Robert has Dallas. I need you to hit up the western cities."

"Okay." He glances over at me as he walks out of the office. "But I shut down online orders. If people want to wait until the last minute they can come into the shop."

Seriously, after I just told him no. I don't argue, though. He's the office manager and knows what he's doing. I want to get them out of here as soon as possible so they have time to spend this day full of love with their respective people.

"Just get going."

I follow him into the warehouse and Xander is

waiting by the door. "I think Caroline is putting the last touches on her niece's flowers. As soon as those are done, I should be good to go."

"Do you have everything loaded?"

"Yep" he nods and gestures to the door, "both vans are ready to go. While Caroline is finishing up, I'll help Kai load whatever car he's taking."

"How did you know he was doing deliveries?"

"His grumpy expression was a good indicator."

"What guy your age describes someone as having a grumpy expression?"

"Um, I do," he grins before opening the door, "it's better than saying he looks bitchy."

It may be better, but I guess both descriptors are accurate. "Okay, y'all." Emily, Sam, and Caroline turn around. "It's getting busy out there. We need to get some premade bouquets together quickly."

"What do you think we've been doing?" Sam points to the ones they've finished on the work table. "It'd go a lot faster if we had all hands on-deck."

"I'm coming." Maybe they'll tell me what they've been scheming for weeks. It's like they try to give Xander and I every opportunity to be alone together. He hasn't even made a move. At least, not since he wanted to grab dinner after the delivery, I went on with him. We're professionals.

The door opens and I glance over my shoulder to see who walked in. It's only my brother stomping his way inside. Okay, maybe one of us is a professional because my eyes land on him anytime he's in the room, and I get a pang of disappointment when he's not.

***

The last of the customers are filing out of the shop. Most shops would stay open until nine on days like today. Not us. Everyone needs to be home in time for dinner. We're already going to have to stay late in a couple of days to prepare for a wedding. The least I can do is make sure these folks get to spend time with their loved ones.

Kai got back from his deliveries about thirty minutes ago. Robert pulled in fifteen minutes ago. Everyone else has been sent home. But Xander still isn't back. I can't even count the number of times he's come back for more orders to deliver in town. These folks seem to want to make sure we keep our lights on.

"Do you want us to wait with you?" Caroline asks as she sweeps the mess on the floor into the dust pan. "It's no biggie."

"Nah," I wave her question away "y'all go ahead and go. I'll finish cleaning up and wait for Xander to get back."

"Are you sure?" Emily moves toward the counter to grab her bag, "I can tell my date to wait."

"You have a date?" Samantha wriggles her eyebrows up and down. "Get it, girl."

Rolling her eyes, she moves toward the door. "Don't get your hopes up. It's just the first date."

"I mean that's all it takes for me." I laugh.

"I'll see y'all tomorrow." She waves and walks out.

Caroline heads in the same direction. "See you later."

"Get out of here, Sam." I shoo her toward the door, "you can go home and watch your love hating movies."

"I was going to do that with or without your permission." She grabs her keys out of her pocket, "have a happy love day."

She doesn't sound excited when she says the last bit. As much as she was a huge part of us setting Caroline up with Carlos, she's as against relationships as I am. But I don't go around watching anti-love movies. I like seeing people getting their happily ever after. It's just not something I want for myself.

Scrolling through my phone, I find my music player and turn on Taylor Swift. If anything, this will make the time fly by as I wait for Xander to get back with the van. There's still a few areas of the shop that need to be cleaned, and I might as well do them now so we come into a clean shop tomorrow.

The counter with the coffee pot is cleared off, and all that's left is the front counter. A part of me wondered if I should have turned the lights off when we closed so people wouldn't try to get in, but it's kind of hard to get anything done in the dark.

Grabbing my phone, I dance my way down the hall and to the store front. The mess up here isn't too bad since all the bouquets were already put together. I pull out the glass cleaner from behind the counter and wipe them down. Too many people have had their germy hands all over them while picking up flowers.

"Kate?" I drop the glass cleaner and jump.

"We'll have to put a bell around you if you keep sneaking up on folks like that." Xander is leaning against the wall where the hall ends. His arms crossed over his chest and his gaze on me.

"I didn't mean to scare you," he uncrosses his arms and holds them up in surrender, "but I wasn't exactly quiet when I came in."

"Sorry, I guess I was too caught up in cleaning and my music."

"Nice choice by the way," he grins, "I wouldn't have pegged you as someone who listens to Swift."

"There's a lot you don't know about me." Crap that's borderline flirting. Get your shit together Kate.

"I see that," he moves toward me and bends down to pick up the cleaner. "I'm guessing everyone else went home?"

"Yep. There wasn't any sense in having everyone stay," I take the cleaner out of his hands and put it back where it belongs. "What took so long with the deliveries?"

"Mr. Jones," Xander groans. "I'm glad I made his delivery last. That man likes to talk."

"Yeah, I guess I should have warned you about him," shaking my head, I grab my phone and move past Xander and down the hallway, "he always has to share some sort of wisdom he's learned in all his years. It's adorable when we aren't trying to get deliveries out."

"He had a lot to say about Valentine's Day and how you should use only this day to show the person you love how much they mean to you." His voice is directly behind me. "He does have solid advice. Kind of reminds me of my parents."

I stop the music on my phone before shoving it in my pocket. "That must be nice."

"I take it your parents don't make out in the middle of the kitchen without caring you're standing two feet away from them?" I turn around to see his expression. His nose is scrunched up in mock disgust. It's sweet his parents are like that. Maybe if mine were, I wouldn't do everything I can to keep from falling for someone.

"You sound like you speak from experience." I laugh and turn off the lights to the store front and hall as soon as he's in the warehouse.

"Almost every single day." He shakes his head and leans against one of the counters. "You'd think I'd be used to it by now, but nope. I have a feeling your parents aren't as affectionate as mine?"

"Not in the slightest." I make another sweep of the warehouse to make sure everything is in its place. "I can count on one hand how many times I've seen them hold hands in public. It's a wonder they ever had kids."

"Maybe they show their affection in other ways. Not everyone is as in your face as my mom and dad. Thank God."

"Maybe," I shrug my shoulders. We need to get off the topic of my parents. Hell, my dad didn't even order flowers for Mom. If he did, it definitely wasn't through us. I kept an eye for his name all day. "Are you ready to get out of here?"

"Yep. But give me just a sec." He rushes past me to the back of the warehouse. I'm not sure what he's doing. I didn't see anything back there when I looked. His steps are slow and measured as he approaches me. He's holding a bouquet of daisies in his hands. "These are for you."

"Y-you shouldn't have."

"I know, but I wanted to." His shoes suddenly interest him, and he doesn't take his focus off of them.

This might be the sweetest thing someone has done for me outside of my friends. Professionalism has flown out the door with us, just as I feared.

"How did you manage to get these without my knowing?"

"Emily wrote it out on the notepad and had me pay in cash so I could surprise you." Now their knowing glances make sense. They have been orchestrating something between me and Xander.

"Of course, she did."

"Are you mad?" His voice cracks.

"Not at all. Thank you, really." I close the distance between us and give him a quick hug. "It's very sweet."

"I also have pizza waiting in the car," he points toward the door. "I didn't know if anyone would be waiting and figured I shouldn't show up empty-handed after the busy day we had."

My stomach growls and I realize I don't remember the last time I even ate. "That actually sounds pretty amazing."

"I can bring it inside, or we can..."

This is going to be a mistake, but right now I don't care. He put in the effort to do something incredibly kind for me. "Why don't you follow me to my apartment? I'm pretty tired of being here."

He moves toward the door, and pushes it open. "After you."

"Actually, after you." I point to the keypad by the door. "I have to set the alarm."

"Oh, right." He walks out of the shop and I know he'll be waiting for me on the other side of the door. Now I only have to remember to keep things friendly, but not too friendly.

xander

EMILY WAS RIGHT. The flowers were a good call. If anyone would know what to do, it's Kate's friends. I get into my car and wait until she walks out of the shop. Once she's safely inside the car and pulling out, I follow behind her.

Honestly, I didn't expect her to be down for dinner. I guess it's a good thing I grabbed the pizza on an off chance that she would. Hopefully she doesn't look too much into the fact that it's shaped as a heart. That wasn't my choice. It was part of a special where I used to work.

What would normally take five minute to get to Kate's apartment, takes closer to fifteen. Cars are out and about for date night and getting last minute gifts for their loved ones. It's a little too late for that in my opinion. The only thing I didn't get is chocolate which is a shame because I know how much she likes it.

She parks in front of her building and I take the spot

next to her. Pushing open the door, I lean out, "Is it okay to park here, or is there a designated spot for guests?"

"You're fine there." She's out of her car and in front of mine, waiting for me to turn it off. "Nobody actually checks to make sure folks are in the right parking areas."

"That's a relief." I turn the car off, and reach over for the pizza. Getting out, I close the door and make my way to Kate. "Why do apartments put that in the rules if they aren't going to enforce it? I had the same experience back at school."

"It's annoying when my neighbors have a ton of people over because I can't park in my normal spot, but they don't give me crap when my friends come over," she shrugs as I follow her up the stairs, "so, I guess it works either way."

"That's something I'll have to look forward to when I find a place." I'm not looking forward to it.

"How's that going, by the way?" We're on the third landing, now. Her apartment is a few doors down.

"I'm still saving money," I wait for her to open it, "figured it would be smarter to have a little nest egg before going out on my own in case anything happens."

She pushes the door open. "That's really smart. Emily, Sam and I shared a place for a long time before all of us got our own places. It was the only way we could afford not to live with our parents."

"I guess it's a good thing y'all get along so well." I wait for her to get inside before closing the door behind me. "If not, it's likely the shop never would have happened."

"Doubtful," she laughs. "The three of us are stubborn. Once we set our minds to something we do it. We would have run the shop together regardless of our liking each other."

"That's commitment." I set the pizza box on the coffee table and take a seat on the couch. Small flashing lights catch my attention. "Hey, the tree is still up, but with different decorations."

"At this point it makes more sense to leave it out and decorate or it for the different seasons."

"Well, it's still a conversation starter." I open the pizza box, "do you have any plates?"

"Yeah, give me just a second." She sets her keys on the countertop and moves toward the kitchen. I hear cabinet doors open and close before water pours from the faucet. She must be putting the flowers in a vase. The water turns off, and there's a scrape against the counter.

Within seconds she's heading back into the living room. Two plates in one hand and a vase in the other. She sets the flowers in the middle of the table and the plates in front of us. "So, was the heart your idea or someone else's?"

I have a feeling she's thinking her friends set up this part. "The restaurants. It's the only ones they are making tonight."

"That's not surprising," she shakes her head and pulls a slice out of the box. They aren't perfect cuts, but it's an odd shape and they did what they could. "Businesses would be dumb not to take advantage of an easy marketing opportunity."

"You're right," I grab a slice. "I don't think I've ever delivered as much as I did today. I know I've never seen that many flowers in twelve-hour period."

"It's our busiest day of the year, along with Mother's Day." She takes a bite and sets the piece back on her plate. "Well, the day before on the last one. I refuse to open on Sundays unless we have a wedding," she stands once more time. "Do you need any ranch or red pepper? I have both."

"No, I'm fine. You don't need to go out of your way."

"I need some for myself, it's not a big deal."

"Red pepper, please." She moves toward the kitchen, "also, do you have anything to drink? I forgot to include drinks in my plan."

"Yeah, I've got water, soda, and sweet tea." For someone who lives by herself she's pretty well stocked. "There's also wine."

"Um, surprise me." Wine doesn't sound like a bad option, but I don't want her thinking I'm up to something. Well, even more than she already knows about. I'm still not sure how she feels about that. She seemed to take it well in the shop.

The fridge opens and I hear her pull glasses down from the cabinet. I feel horrible for not helping, but I don't know where anything is...yet.

Kate comes back in the living room with a bottle of wine and two glasses. "There isn't much left, but I'm certain we can finish it off."

"It's over half a bottle." How is that not much?

"True. But there are two of us, and I'm not used to sharing."

"You've got a point." I grab the bottle and pull the cork out before pouring a small amount in both glasses.

"You might as well go ahead and add more to that cup."

"I thought it was only supposed to be filled a small portion at a time."

"That's for people who drink wine like you're supposed to," she holds the glass in front of me, "I'm not one of those people."

"Okay." I fill her glass a little over half way. "Is it too early for infomercials to be on?"

She laughs and almost spits out her wine. "Definitely. They don't come on until way later. Do you want to watch a movie?"

"If you want to." I hope she says yes because the small moments of silence are kind of unsettling. Filling the awkward pauses isn't in my skillset. The chatter between us ebbed and flowed last time we were in this position. Now it feels odd because I'm trying my hardest not to overstep any boundaries.

"Definitely." She grabs the remote and sits closer to me than she was before. "Even though it was a long day, I'm not nearly tired enough to try going to sleep."

"I understand that. I'm just happy to be out of the van." I slide my shoes off and push them aside with my feet. "I don't think I ever felt that way delivering pizzas. But it's probably because today was full of going back and forth."

"Yeah, it can take a lot out of you. I don't know how the four of us did it on our own." She turns on the TV and clicks to one of the streaming channels. "It probably helped we didn't have the attention we do now. Anything in particular you want to watch?"

She switches topics so fast sometimes it's hard to keep up. "Um, it doesn't matter. I'm not picky."

"Seriously?" She's shocked at my answer. "You'd be okay if I put on a Romcom or something super romantic?"

"Yep." I shrug and lean into the couch. "I'm used to watching movies with my parents. My mom loves romance and my dad loves action movies. I watch whatever they want to watch, and when they go to bed, I turn on cheesy sci-fi."

The moment the words leave my mouth, I cringe. That makes me sound pathetic. Instead of going out all the time, I choose to hang out with my parents, watching movies.

"That's actually pretty cool." She shakes her head, "I wish I could do things like that with my parents. Now that I think about it, I don't think I've ever watched a movie with them."

"It may not be a bad thing. It can get uncomfortable with some of the stuff my mom watches." A shiver runs through my body. "Seeing sex scenes isn't something I should be a part of when my mom is in the room."

"At least she's not ashamed of what she likes." Kate scrolls through the selections before clicking on a movie that was made way before me. I think my mom has watched it, but I know I've never seen it.

"True." Leaning forward I grab my glass of wine. "Honestly, I'm surprised you like romance movies. Don't you dislike relationships?"

Her cheeks blush at the question. "I dislike relationships for *me*. I love it for everyone else."

"Really?" That's actually pretty weird. But good to know she's not against just relationships. She only refuses to let herself fall into one.

"Yep. Nothing makes me happier than when friends, or people I know, fall in love," she points the remote toward the TV before setting it down, "it's like watching one of these movies and fills me with nothing but joy."

"So why don't you want it for you?" It's a valid question.

"Because my parents didn't show any ounce of affection toward each other my entire life. My dad takes his role as man of the house to the next level. Don't get me wrong, he's not abusive toward my mom or anything, but he's just not a super fun person. I'm honestly terrified that's how all relationships end up."

"Okay, that makes some sort of sense. But what about your friends?" I turn toward her, studying her emotions, "you can see they aren't in the same situation. So, it's possible for you to have a normal, healthy relationship."

"They mostly grew up with at least one loving parent."

"What about your brother? He has a girlfriend, right?"

She scrunches up her nose. "He doesn't count. He's always been the golden child. Everything comes easily to him and he can do no wrong."

"Woah, don't sell having a sibling too hard." It's something I've always wanted, and even though my parents wanted more kids, it just didn't happen.

"No, it's nothing like that. I love my brother. He's in my inner circle of best friends. But the way my parents treat him versus how they treat me is visible to everyone. Ask the girls. They've seen it our entire lives. Even Kai knows even though he acts like he doesn't."

It seems like she's been holding that in for a while. I'm sure her friends know all about it, how could they not? But it's definitely a perspective I never thought about.

"Is it because he's younger?"

She taps her fingers on her leg. "Maybe? I don't know. It could be because he doesn't put up much of a fight when he doesn't agree with something our parents are saying. He lets it go." She grins and glances over at me. "That's something I've never been able to do. Most of the time whatever I think pops out of my mouth."

Huh, I can see that in most aspects except where I'm concerned. She seems to be pretty tight lipped about anything involving me. I want to say the words so badly, but I keep my mouth shut. This is one of those moments where I need to let her lead the way. Emily would be so proud of me.

"That makes sense." I glance at the movie we've all but forgotten about, "I think we may need to restart it. I have no idea what's going on."

"We can watch something else," she grabs the remote again, "Caroline's mom showed us this movie one night at a sleepover. We were like fifteen, I think."

"I'm fine with watching this."

"No, it's fine. I kind of don't want to watch it anymore," she holds the remote in front of me. "Why don't you pick one of those cheesy sci-fi movies. I can honestly say I've never really watched one."

"Oh, um, sure." I grab the remote and flip through the categories. I don't want to pick something she's going to make fun of. Though, that's pretty difficult. There. This one shouldn't be too bad. These people are stuck on a planet and are attacked by aliens in the dark. There's only one person who can see them to fight them off.

The opening scenes flash across the TV. "This looks... interesting. Let me turn off the light."

Chuckling, I shake my head. This woman truly is something else.

I MOVE and realize I'm on the edge of the sofa. Glancing up Xander is slumped in the corner. My head is in his lap and I'm lying across the whole sofa. That can't be comfortable for him. I can't believe we both fell asleep.

Shifting my weight, I roll off the sofa. A quick glance at my phone shows it's just after midnight. Both of us must have been exhausted because I don't think we finished the movie. The TV is stuck on the recommendation page based on the movie we just watched.

My knees pop as I stand up, but Xander doesn't budge. At least he's not a light sleeper. I can't leave him like that, though. His back will be yelling at him later. I gently shake his leg, hoping that will stir him awake. It doesn't. I push a little harder, waiting for any sort of reaction. Still nothing.

Leaning down, I brace myself against the back of the

sofa. "Xander," I whisper close to his ear while shaking his shoulder. "Xander." This time a little louder.

He sits up and almost bumps his head against mine. "Woah."

"Hey, we fell asleep," I take a step back, "it's after midnight. But you looked really uncomfortable, and I didn't want to leave you like that."

"Oh, sorry," he rubs his hand over his face, "I didn't mean to fall asleep. I'll, uh, go."

"You don't have to leave." I place a hand on his arm. "You can take the couch...or sleep in the bed."

I can't believe I just offered that. It's not something I've ever done before, but it appears I'm doing lots of things that are out of character when it comes to Xander. He makes me feel things I never thought I'd want for myself. It's not because he's pushed me into having feelings for him, either. It's the little things. The way he brings donuts for everyone. Or goes out of his way to make sure I have flowers for Valentine's Day. Nobody I've known has ever done that for me before.

He glances up at me, trying to read my expression. "Are you sure? I don't want to make things weird."

"I wouldn't have said it if I wasn't sure." That's a lie. It popped out of my mouth. I really need to learn to keep my inside thoughts...inside.

"Okay," he stands, and puts his hand out to mine, "as long as you're sure."

"Yeah, it's totally fine." I place my hand in his and lead him toward the bedroom. "I mean, we're both adults." Which explains the very adult thoughts going through my mind.

He follows after me, and I turn on the light as we come into my room. I'm trying so hard to keep this from being awkward, but I don't know if I can do that. His body is rigid and I think he can feel it, too.

"Same side as last time?" He nods toward the side closest to the wall. We didn't really establish sides the last time he was here. He followed my lead and waited until I laid down on the side I usually sleep on. That side of the bed faces the window, and I leave the blinds cracked so if I miss my alarm at least the sun will wake me up by shining in my face.

"Uh, sure." I let go of his hand and move toward my dresser. "I think Kai may have left some sweatpants when he was sleeping on my sofa over Christmas."

"Oh, no. It's fine, I can sleep in my clothes." He's had those on all day through multiple deliveries. There's no way he's going to be comfortable.

"Yeah, I don't think so." I continue digging through a drawer and find the pants my brother left. "Here," I toss them at him, "I'm gonna go get in my jammies."

"I wasn't aware you wore them." Smart ass. Last time I didn't because we were otherwise occupied. The grin on his face is adorable and infuriating. There's no way I'm keeping up this barrier between us, and the more time I spend with him, I'm not sure I want to.

"Well," I huff, "I do. Now, if you'll excuse me."

I grab the clothes out of my drawer and slam it closed before heading to the bathroom. It's not like I wear fancy pajamas. It's literally old college shirts and shorts. I don't care how cold it is outside, it's what I wear to bed every single night. I've never really seen the point in wearing something fancy when I'm the only one who sees them. At least in a t-shirt and shorts, I'm comfortable.

Taking my time, I remove my makeup and wash my face. Now that I think about it, I don't think he's ever seen me without makeup. Hell, even when I woke up late that morning, I still had it on. It may not have been pretty, but it was there. Will he think differently of me when I'm not wearing it. This is the problem with being attracted to a man younger than me. My insecurities scream at me from every direction, and I don't know how to shut them up.

I switch clothes and toss the ones I wore today in the hamper. It feels good to be out of them. As much as I love what Valentine's Day does for business, I hate how gross I feel afterward. My jammies would have been on as soon as I walked in the door if Xander hadn't come home with me.

One, two, three deep breaths and I open the bath-room door. Xander's clothes are in a neat pile next to the nightstand with his shoes sitting beside them. He's on the same side he slept on last time. His bare chest peeking out from under the comforter. Good gravy, I could get used to that sight. The TV is on and informer-cials flash across the screen.

"Sorry, I can turn it off," he grabs the remote. "I just felt weird lying here with absolutely nothing to do. Also,

I may get one of those things that vacuum and mop at the same time for my mom's birthday."

"So, they do work." I laugh and hurry to my side of the bed. "Who would have thought these late-night commercials would actually entice you to buy something."

He mumbles something under his breath, but I can't hear most of it. I catch, "kept my mind off something else." He hands me the remote to change the channel. "She always complains about having to do both at different times. This is a way to make things easier for her, especially once I move out."

"That's pretty sweet." I honestly couldn't tell you want my parents complain about. I avoid them as much as I can. No doubt they would find something I'm doing wrong, and I don't want to give them the opportunity. They should not take up so much of my energy. I'm a grown ass woman, but old habits die hard, I guess.

"Thanks. I like to think I'm a sweet person." He nods toward the hallway. "I mean, I did bring pizza and flowers."

"That you did," I reach over and grab his hand, "thank you."

"It really wasn't a big deal," he squeezes my hand and doesn't let go. "You deserve something nice, especially on chaotic as hell days."

He's the first person that has gone out of his way to do something for me outside of my friend group. Even the boyfriends I had in high school, and the few in college never did anything groundbreaking. Hell, I was lucky if they covered dinner.

"It was to me." I click the power button on the remote and set it on my nightstand without letting go of his hand. Rolling over I fluff my pillow with my free hand and wrap his arm around my waist. "Good night."

"Night, Kate." He follows my lead, no questions asked. This feels nice. It's comforting in a way I never expected.

His thumb rubs along the elastic of my shorts. Unsure of whether it's meant to turn me on, or meant to soothe me, I don't move. As much as I want him to go lower, I'm going to let him make the first move. I kind of took over the entire situation last time. It'll be nice to see if he has the initiative to do it now. All these weird out of character feelings I'm having need to go away. I really don't have time for this with everything happening at the shop.

He scoots closer to me until my back is against his chest. His arms encompasses my entire body and he pulls even closer to him. "Is this okay?" His voice is a light whisper against my ear, and my entire body reacts.

"Uh huh." He makes me feel things I've never felt before. The need to get to know him outside of the bedroom, but the way my body syncs to his so perfectly is telling.

He moves his hand until his fingers slide under the waistband of my shorts and panties. His thumb caressing my skin as his fingers inch lower and lower. My breath hitches as he brushes against my clit before sinking a finger into me. He's taking his time and its tortuous pleasure.

His lips trail kisses along my neck as his thumb circles my clit and two fingers pump into me. Never has a man given me this much attention without me doing anything in return. The buzz building through my body is making me antsy. I slide my foot along his leg, needing to move in some way an open my legs wider, giving him better access.

Sliding my arm between us, I awkwardly reach for the waistband of his pants. Doing nothing while he does all the work isn't fair to him, but I'm not exactly in the best position to participate. As much as I want to take control of the situation, I don't.

Xander moves from behind me and I roll over onto my back as he hovers over me. His fingers still working magic between my legs and his lips never leaving my neck. He kisses his way up until his lips meet mine. There are still too many clothes between us and I pull the bottom of my shirt up until I can feel his chest against my breasts.

The friction as I rock in rhythm to his fingers is almost more than I can take. He breaks the kiss and his lips trail down my neck until his lips wrap around my nipple while his free hand pinches the other between two fingers. I gasp at the pain but relish in it. The sensation is overwhelming and I'm unsure what to do. He's hitting every one of my sensitive spots at the same time.

My fingers slide into his hair and grip as I pull his lips further into me. His tongue swirls around my nipple before biting lightly and releasing me. His lips begin a path lower and his slides his fingers out of me to pull down my shorts and panties. I don't know how much more of this teasing I can take. As much as I like foreplay, I'm not used to *this* much attention.

I watch him as he slides my clothes down my legs and tosses them behind him. His eyes are focused on me as his tongue circles my clit and I buck at the contact. His arm goes over my waist keeping me in place as he goes down on me. I grab onto the sheets because I'm afraid if I grab his hair again, I may pull too hard. His eyes never leave mine as he brings me closer and closer to the edge.

I wrap my legs over his shoulders, trying to bring him closer to me. Closer to the release I know is coming. They tighten as energy buzzes through me and I come. He doesn't stop, though. His mouth continues moving until my legs are shaking, and I don't know if I'll be able to walk when he's done.

Sitting up he pushes his pants down his legs and reaches into the drawer he knows holds the condoms I keep on hand. "Do you want me to stop?" His voice is deep and raspy.

"No," mine is breathless and needy as I pull my shirt over my head and toss it to the floor, "I need you, Xander."

And it's not a lie. Right now, in this moment, I need to feel all of him. The terrifying thing is I think I may need him to stick around outside of the bedroom. He makes me feel like an entirely different woman. One who wants all those things some of my friends have with their partners. Tonight, changes everything.

CHAPTER TWELVE

xander

THIS IS a new experience for me. Not waking up in Kate's bed, but not being rushed out of it. Last time I stayed over she was practically kicking me out of her apartment. This time...it's different. Her alarm is going off on her phone, and she's not budging.

I gently shake her shoulders. Still not budging. I doubt she'll be getting glammed up for today, unless she has a meeting. But I don't remember seeing anything on the white board. Either way, she has time to sleep a little longer.

As quietly as possible, I slide out from under the comforter. I glance around the area; I know the sweatpants I borrowed are here somewhere. I'm not sure I'm at the comfort level to be walking around her apartment in my birthday suit. What if someone comes by, or can see in the windows?

Finally, I see them lying by the dresser on the opposite side of the room, and hurry toward them. How they ended up over here, I have no idea. Well, I do, but that's beside the point. I slip them on, and tiptoe out of the room.

I've never been in her kitchen, but I know she lives off coffee at the shop. I search through the cabinets until I finally find one with all her coffee making stuff. It's weird it's not on the counter, but to each their own. Filling the reservoir with water, I place the pod into the coffee maker. Crap. What if she doesn't have any creamer? Oh well, I guess we'll find out in a bit.

I search for the coffee mugs, and place it under the coffee maker. Pressing the button, I turn toward the fridge. Maybe she has something to cook for breakfast. As soon as I open the door, I stand in shock. The only contents are creamer, a tub of butter and a tray of fruit that looks like it's about to grow something. At least I know she has the stuff she needs for the coffee. But seriously, what does she eat? There's literally nothing here.

The freezer may hold better options. I open the door and there's a least a little bit of food in here. Most notable are the waffles shoved into a corner. That will work. Pulling the box out, I set it on the counter next to the toaster. We'll make do with what she has. All I see are signs that she works way too much. Or, she doesn't regularly shop for groceries. Her food situation looks like mine and my roommates in college. For us, it was because we were broke. There's a huge different.

"Please tell me that's coffee and I'm not dreaming." Kate trudges into the kitchen with her robe wrapped tight around her.

"You aren't dreaming," I laugh. "I figured you could use a few more minutes of sleep. So, I put your coffee on and looked for food. By the way, when was the last time you went to the store?"

She looks around the room as if that's going to give her all the answers she's looking for. "I actually don't know. We've been so busy at the shop I've been living off takeout."

"Clearly," I mumble, "maybe you should do that on Sunday since the shop is closed."

"Probably." She agrees. She moves next to me and pulls the mug toward her. "It's not my favorite thing to do. It takes up so much time, and the last thing I want to do on my day off is spend it doing adult things."

"You can always schedule a pick up or have it delivered." Both of these options have saved me more times than I can count. Well, my mom anyway. She doesn't like running errands on the weekend either.

"Good point." She moves around the kitchen getting things together for her coffee. "Wow, you actually found food in there?" She points to the box of waffles.

"Yeah, I found food." One set of waffles pops out of the toaster. "Here you go." I set them on a paper towel. I don't know where the plates are, and I have no idea if she even has the stuff to top them. From the contents of her fridge, I doubt it.

"Thanks for letting me sleep." She takes a sip of her coffee now that it's to her taste. Honestly, it's best described as creamer with a splash of coffee. "I don't remember the last time I've done that. Also, a good thing we are opening late today."

"That was a smart move. Everyone needs a little rest after yesterday." I glance down at my borrowed pants. "It also gives me time to go home and get ready before I head back to the shop."

Kate takes another sip of her coffee, glancing at me over the rim of her mug. "About that."

Nothing good ever comes from those two words. "Yeah?"

"I want to see what is building between us, but I don't necessarily want to flaunt it in front of the rest of the team."

"So, you want to keep this," I point between me and her, "a secret?"

She rubs a hand over her face. "That came out wrong. Not really a secret, more like not showing any sort of PDA at work. My best friends and brother can of course know what the deal is. But everybody else, I don't think it would be a good idea."

"Um, okay." I'm not exactly sure what I'm supposed to say to that. I don't really understand the need to keep things a secret from anyone. As she said, we're both adults. If other people have a problem with it, that's something they need to deal with. "I just don't under-stand what the big deal is."

"It's not. Or, it shouldn't be. But just for a little bit." She runs a hand through her hair. "It's not for a long time, just long enough to make sure we're going to work, and it won't affect everyone at the shop."

"You realize that pretty much leaves four people that can't know, right? It's pointless to do that."

"Then we keep it a secret from everyone." She's dead set on doing this.

"For how long?" Before I even think about agreeing to this, I need to know the parameters she's wanting to set up. It's not exactly fair for me to be her dirty little secret.

"I don't know," she shrugs and takes a sip of her coffee, "just until we can figure out how everyone will react to us."

It's a copout, and can be see a mile away. But I also know she doesn't typically do relationships. If I really want to see where things could go with us, I need to meet her halfway. This is new territory for her. Not only with the relationship, but with opening up to someone for more than one night. A million reasons why I shouldn't agree to this fly through my head, but I push them aside. Kate is worth this minor inconvenience to get to know on a deeper level.

"Okay." I begin cleaning up the small mess I made while making her waffles. "As long as it's not forever, I think I can handle that."

"Really?" The shock in her voice forces me to turn in her direction. "Most guys would have run miles away."

"There's one thing you should know about me, Kate," I move toward her and slide my finger under her chin, "I'm not most guys."

After a quick peck on the lips, I move around her and walk to the bedroom. Let her think over those words for a moment. Even though the shop is opening late today, I still need to go home and get ready. I doubt we'll be busy with deliveries, but I know the shop is going to need major cleaning after the chaos from yesterday.

The parking lot to the shop is empty, aside from one car, when I pull in. I guess everyone else will get here at the last possible second. Honestly, I probably would be too, but I can't handle being late to a shift. It's just not how I operate.

The door to the warehouse area is unlocked and I walk in. Kate is standing by one of the shelves with a tablet in her hand. I wonder how much earlier she got here than I did. The inventory is being taken for what we have left after the sales yesterday. There also looks to be a couple of vases on the delivery shelf. I guess a few people decided they wanted to get some flower orders in late. Or, they'd rather not deal with the rush.

"Busy day today?" I move to her side.

"Not really," she points at the bottom shelf, "we got a few orders in late last night for today, but other than that. It'll be taking inventory and helping walk-ins."

"Do you need some help with inventory?" My shoulder brushes against hers as I peek at the tablet, and her entire body shivers. "It would probably go faster with two people."

A few seconds pass as she gets herself under control. "Do you know all the flowers by sight?"

Of course, she'd ask that. "Um, not yet. But I know some of them."

"Then I think I've got this." She smirks at me, and I'll now make it my mission to know as many of the flowers as possible.

My hand drifts to her side, and I run my fingers along her waist where a sliver of skin is showing. "We could find other ways to fill the time before the work day starts."

"What if someone comes in?" She glances over my shoulder. "We're supposed to keep this under wraps."

Shrugging, I lean in closer to her. My finger sliding into the belt loop on her pants, pulling her closer to me. "That door is loud as hell. The minute someone begins pulling it open, it'll creak." She's nervous, and I don't blame her. This is probably so far out of her wheelhouse she doesn't know how to react. "We could always *count inventory* in the back of the shop. Then nobody would catch the slightest glimpse of us."

Instead of answering, she slips out of my grasp and grabs my hand, leading me to the back shelves where there's more cover. I don't say anything, and let her take the lead. We come to a stop along between the last shelves and the wall. Nobody will be able to see us if they walk through the warehouse door. Not even if they come through the front door and through the all. Not that I've ever seen anyone do that. But there's a first time for everything.

Kate sets the tablet on an empty section of the shelf and throws her arms around my neck before her lips crash into mine. It's good to know she's been antsy since we parted ways this morning. She's all I thought about since the moment I left her apartment. If I'm being honest, she hasn't left my mind for weeks.

Her fingers dig into my hair and she deepens the kiss. Our tongues twirling and I turn her around until her back is against the shelf. I grab the one above me to keep my balance because everything about this woman throws me off in the best way possible.

My arm wraps around her waist and I lift her up, her legs hooking around mine. Our kiss intensifies and she's rocking into me. This woman is going to make it hard for me to walk out of these shelves without anyone noticing what we were doing.

A soft moan escapes her lips and I melt at the sound. We should stop. I know that, but it's so hard to pull away from her. The chemistry we have together is unlike anything I've ever felt. Not that I've had a ton of relationships, but nothing has come even close to comparison. Kate makes me feel alive when we're together.

One of her hands moves to the waist of my jeans, toying with the button. Holy shit, are we going to do this here of all places. After she said being together at work is off limits. She's leading the way, though.

She gets them unbuttoned and slides her hand toward my underwear.

"Hello?" Her hand stills and she moves away from my mouth. "Kate? Xander? Are you here?"

"Fuck," Kate whispers against my lips. Both of us were so caught up in each other we didn't hear the door open. Maybe she was right about us not being public while at work. The position we're in at this very moment is comprising.

She unhooks her legs and slides them down my body before straightening her shirt. Running her hands through her hair, she smooths out the tendrils that were coming out of her ponytail. One piece is falling over her face and I move it behind her ear.

"I'm sorry." I take a step back giving her space to make sure she's presentable.

"No, it's fine. I take all the blame on this one." She waits for me to button my jeans and messes with my hair until it doesn't look like she's been gripping it in her hands. "Can you hand me the tablet?"

"Guys," Emily's voice sounds closer than it was before. "Where are y'all?"

"Back here," Kate calls in response, "showing Xander the flowers so he can help with inventory."

"Ugh, inventory sucks." Emily groans, but I hear her steps closer to us. She comes to a stop when she sees the both of us facing the shelf. "I brought breakfast burritos if y'all want any."

"Thanks." I rush around her and toward the front of the room. I do not need to give away that we're together, and sticking around will do just that. I have a tendency to wear my heart on my sleeve. And my expressions say everything I'm trying to hide.

The two of them start whispering as I make my way down the aisle. I'm almost positive Emily knows something is up. So much for keeping things a secret at work.

I DIDN'T REALIZE how hard it was going to be working with Xander. Not because he's a bad employee or anything. But because I can't stop thinking about him. He occupies my thoughts at home, at work, and anytime I'm trying to keep him out of my mind. It never seems to work. Who is this woman I'm becoming?

"Are you ready for your appointment, Kate?" Kai calls from the office.

"Huh?" My focus is solely on Xander, who happens to be loading deliveries for this afternoon. I think we're going out later tonight, but in the city so nobody catches on that we're dating. It's been a couple of weeks, and aside from Emily sniffing around, nobody else has mentioned anything.

"Your bridal appointment," Kai is now in front of me at the workstation, "the ping should have gone off for you an hour ago. She'll be here in fifteen minutes."

Crap. I silenced the notification as soon as it went off.

Glancing at the whiteboard, I notice it isn't on there. That's why I like the manual system. It's in my face at all times, and I don't have to have my phone on me.

"Sorry. I was trying to finish up this order." My words are rushed and I don't know that I'm actually fooling anyone.

He glances over at me and the direction my body is facing, then at the bouquet I've been working on for the past thirty minutes. Honestly, it shouldn't be taking me this long, but I keep getting distracted. "If you say so," he points to the office, "I already have her information pulled up on the computer. Go familiarize yourself with it. I'll get Samantha to finish up this arrangement so it can go out the door."

"You've got it." I fight the urge to look over my shoulder toward Xander as I hurry down the hallway to the office. The last thing I need is for my brother to put the pieces together. I don't think he'd be upset that we're dating, but he won't be a fan of the fact I've been lying to him about it.

He was right about having the information pulled up. But I can already tell based on the general interests this client will be a handful. I usually work with the wedding planner, but so many people are doing it themselves these days and that means I have to talk directly to the bride.

I glance over the information one more time and note that she doesn't have a planner listed. Great. Reaching into the desk drawer, I pull out a notepad and set it on the desk in front of me. I'll add it to her info card later.

Writing it out by hand is the fastest way for me to get down information.

There's a knock at the office door, and Kai is standing there with two women. "Kate this is Shelby, the bride and her wedding planner, Angela."

Standing, I reach a hand out to both of them. "I'm Kate. It's nice to meet you." I'm also grateful she does have a planner. It means most of my contact with go through her. "Please, have a seat." I motion to the chairs in front of the desk.

Ugh when we remodel, we need to add an area specifically for meetings. Being in this cramped office is embarrassing. Ideally, I would love something a little sleeker and that has fewer files and filing cabinets against all the walls.

"I heard your flower shop is handling the florals for Crooked Halo's manager." Shelby leans forward and barely refrains from blasting her hands together.

"Yes, we are," I nod in answer, "but I can't share any details per our contract." That's a lie, but it keeps people from asking personal questions. Tiffany and Spencer refused to sign anything. They basically told me to do what I wanted. It's actually kind of annoying.

"I mean," Shelby grins, "if they have faith in you to make their wedding beautiful, then so do I."

"Do you have any idea what color schemes you want? Or what types of flowers?" These are the two questions I always start with. It gives me an idea of where to lead the brides.

"I think soft and romantic." She stares into space.

"Or, maybe even fun and flirty." Great, she has no clue. "We haven't really talked about it."

Her wedding planner rolls her eyes. I feel the same way except I can't actually do anything about it. "Let's see what we can work through and go from there."

Angela pulls out a binder and sets it on the desk. There aren't a ton of notes on the pages, and I lose all hope this is going to be an easy wedding. It would have been nice if there was some sort of prep work, but it's something I'll have to work through. Angela glances at me and forces a smile. She likely hasn't had an easy time of it either. "Let's start from the beginning."

It's going to be such a long day. Thank God I have plans tonight to make it better.

***

"Rough day?" Xander asks as soon as he sees me walk out the door. He's already walking my way from his car. I peek around to make sure everyone else left.

"How long have you been standing out here?" I don't need him blowing our cover within the first couple of weeks.

He takes a step back and holds his hands up. "I left and came back once I figured everyone else was gone."

"Oh," my shoulders sag in relief. That's good to know. "Sorry, it's been...a day. I swear if my brother gives me another appointment with a bride who doesn't know what she wants, I'm going to lose it."

"I thought that was something most people dream

about since they were little." Ugh, men. "At least, that's what they show in the movies."

The wind whips around us, and I gather my hair in one hand to keep it from hitting me in the face. I'll be happy when the weather is warmer and this stormy season goes away. "Not all kids do that. I didn't."

"Yeah, but you had a very different upbringing with your parents." He wraps an arm around my waist and leads us to his car. "A lot of people have parents that make out in front of them."

"No offense," I slap his chest, "but I don't think most people have parents like that. Yours are just ridiculously in love."

"I swear they are like those cheesy TV couples. It's adorable and terrifying all at the same time." He opens the passenger door and waits until I'm inside before going around the front and sliding in behind the wheel. "But I think I want that for myself. I can't imagine being with someone for the rest of my life that didn't show any sort of affection."

The words are a punch to the gut. He didn't mean to direct them toward me, but it hits me all the same. He deserves someone who will love him the way he says his parents love each other. I just don't know if I can be that for him. I mean, it's all fun right now, but I'm also keeping him a secret from all our friends and coworkers. How is that fair to him?

"Hey, are you okay?" He glances at me as he turns on the car and puts it in gear.

"Yeah, I'm fine. It's just been a long day," I slide my hand into his, "I'm ready for it to be over."

He gives my hand a tight squeeze. "We don't have to go out if you don't want to. I can take you home and let you get some rest."

"Do I look that exhausted?" Gah, I hope not.

"Not at all, you just sound defeated," he puts the car back in park. "If rest is something you need more, then you should take it." Turning his entire body toward me, he lifts his free hand and runs it along my chin. "I don't want to be a reason you don't get the rest you need or deserve. I will be fine, and you don't have to worry about us."

The feeling he puts behind those words make my heart melt. That is how I know he deserves someone who can love him the way he needs. There aren't many people who will put their needs and wants aside to make sure someone else is okay. Hell, even my own parents don't do that. He truly is one of the best people I know.

"Are you sure? I know we've had this planned, but right now I kind of want to go home and go to sleep."

"Absolutely," he nods, "do you want me to drive you home? It's a little windy for you to be walking. Being sick on top of dealing with brides who don't know what they want isn't exactly the best combination."

"That would be great." How did I get so lucky? Though if I wasn't seeing him, I wouldn't have anyone to vent to other than my brother and friends. They would tell me to suck it up and get over it. Well, maybe not Caroline or Emily, but the other two would for sure.

I lean the seat back and stare out the window. The drive won't take very long, but it's nice to not have to worry about getting home. The wind is whipping through the trees and the light poles seem to be bending the slightest bit. Xander was right to suggest brining me home. I need to get over myself and drive more often, but I can't justify it when I live so close to the shop.

Within minutes we are pulling into the parking lot of my apartment. He parks next to my car and puts his in park. "Do you want me to walk you up?"

"No, I'll be fine." I move the seat back into sitting position and lean over the console to give him a kiss. He lifts his hand to gently cup my cheek and now I wish more than anything we were going out. But I can barely keep my eyes open. His lips are a whisper against mine. The tenderness is completely opposite from any other exchange we've ever had. Even our kissing has been full of passion and fire, but this is warmth and love. Something I'm starting to feel to my very core.

"Are you sure?"

"Yeah, I've got it." Before he has a chance to open the door for me, I do it and step out of the car. "See you tomorrow, Xan."

"Night, Kate." With that I close the door behind me and trudge up the stairs to my apartment.

The tree is still lit up with Valentine's decorations in the corner of my living room. Guess I forgot to turn it off last night. I drop my bag on the floor, lock the door behind me and head to my room. My first priority is a shower to wash away the day's frustration. I still can't believe a bride came to me without knowing anything about what she wants. Those meetings usually only take about an hour, this one took three. Kai was getting antsy waiting for us to leave his sanctuary in the office.

I don't take a long shower. I'm honestly too tired for that, but my stomach grumbles and I really need to eat something. As I'm walking into the living room, there's a knock on my door. Xander is the only person it can be. My heart skips a beat that he didn't take no for an answer.

Glancing through the peephole, the butterflies in my stomach come to a halt. It's not Xander, but a person holding a box is standing in front of my door. I unlock it and open it partially. "Can I help you?"

"Yeah, uh, you're Kate, right?" He glances at a piece of paper on top of the pizza box in his hands.

"Yes," I draw out, "but I didn't order anything."

"Xander called in the order and wanted me to make sure you got it." Always thinking of my well-being. He may not have shown up in person, but he has his ways of showing he cares.

"Oh," I open the door wider to take the box. It's cold outside, and I'm only in a robe. "Thank you. Hold on, let me grab some cash from my bag."

"No worries," he holds his hands up, "Xander took care of all of it."

"Thanks. Be careful in that wind."

"Yes, ma'am." I close the door as soon as he turns. I'm nowhere near old enough to be called ma'am. It's a respect thing, I know that. But at the same time, does it really need to be said?

Grabbing my phone from my bag, I shoot off a text to Xander.

KATE

Thank you.

XANDER

So you got the food? I didn't know if you'd gone grocery shopping and wanted to make sure you ate.

KATE

Yes. You're turning out to be a prince.

XANDER

I'm okay with that. Night.

I don't bother texting back because it will defeat the purpose of me falling asleep. But I need to make it up to him. Maybe we'll have our date night tomorrow night. Surely the girls will understand if I skip a girls' night out.

xander

WHO KNEW GETTING a pizza delivered would equate to being princely? Kate is opening up more and more to me every day. I can only hope soon we'll be able to be a couple in front of our coworkers. I'm almost certain Emily knows something is up. She keeps staring at me and Kate when she thinks we're not paying attention.

"Hey, you ready for these deliveries?" Robert asks as I'm watching Kate across the room. She does look better than she did last night. There's a new energy about her and I'd like to think I had something to do with that.

"Yep." I grab one of the bouquets and load it into his van. "It looks like you've got the West side of the city and I have the East." I glance at the delivery papers and groan. "And it looks like one of mine is a funeral."

"Better you than me," Robert chuckles, "but if you need me to do it, I can."

"No, I'll be fine." It's not a lie, but funerals make me

uncomfortable. I haven't been to many. Most of my relatives are still alive and well, and I've never experienced a loss close to me. At least it's the first delivery of the day and I can get it over with. Hopefully, I won't run into any of the grieving family. Awkward is probably the best description when I'm placed in uncomfortable situations.

Before long both of our vans are loaded. The last thing is this wreath for the funeral. Ugh I really don't want to do that stop. Robert and I load the wreath in the back of the van closest to the doors. It's the first stop and nobody wants to dig around for flowers.

As soon as I close the doors, I head toward the wall with the key hooks. Except the key to the van, I usually take isn't there. Robert is waving the keys in his hand and gets in the driver seat. "Sorry, kid. I can't do that to you."

"Thanks, Man." I wave as he drives off. I don't know what I did to deserve that, but whatever it is, I'm grateful. I grab the other keys and head toward the van.

"I thought you had the East side today." Kate leans against the delivery shelf.

"I did, but as soon as Robert realized I had to deliver to a funeral home, he switched vans." Shrugging my shoulders, I unlock the door. I really need to get on the road if I want to get back at a decent time. I'm not sure what she has planned for tonight, but if she's busy I may go out.

"That was sweet of him." A small smile graces her face, and I know she means it. "I didn't mean to give you the funeral, but you were already going to be in the area."

"When y'all started, how did you handle areas and situations you weren't comfortable with?" It's something I've wondered because I'm sure they've had to deal with some wild situations.

"We did our job. We didn't really have a choice." She walks toward me and stops inches from the open door. She really is pressing her luck with people finding out about us. They have to be curious about why she spends so much time around me. "If we didn't make the deliveries, or deal with the asshole customers, we didn't get paid. And if we didn't get paid, we couldn't make the rent. There was no way in hell I was asking my parents for help."

I can't really blame her, but her pride is what is going to be her downfall. There are other ways she can ask for help outside her parents. Though, I'm sure Kai fills them in on things when they want to know something.

"Makes sense." I climb into the van and wait for Kate to scoot back before I close the door. "I better go if I want to be back before the shop closes."

"See you later." She waves at me before I have a chance to get out of the driveway she yells out, "What are you are doing tonight?"

Of course, she'd ask that as I'm driving off instead of when I'm right next other her. Maybe this means we get a chance to make up for last night.

She never texted me back after I asked her what she had in mind. Her car also isn't in the parking lot when I get to the shop. Maybe I did something wrong? It's odd for her to leave me hanging for this long. Normally, she responds right away. Unless, of course, she's busy. Which happens a lot. Especially now that wedding season is ramping up. I don't think I've seen them all this stressed since we were delivering for Valentine's Day.

I back the van to the door, put it in park and get ready to clean it out. A small part of me wants to put it off until the morning but I don't want to leave the vehicle Robert usually takes messy. He could potentially come in early in the morning and I don't want him cleaning up after me.

"What took so long?" Kai opens the back door and slides a brick in front of it to hold it open. "Everyone else is already gone, or getting ready to go."

Well, that answers my question about Kate. "Traffic. I don't know what is in the air today it felt like nobody remembers how to drive without being a jerk."

He smirks as he opens the van door, "And that is why I'm glad I don't do deliveries anymore. Dealing with people was the easy part, but sitting in traffic...not fun at all."

"Traffic doesn't usually bother me, but today was a nightmare on the road." I sweep the fallen leaves and petals into a pile. "Where did everyone go? And why are you the only person I see here?"

That may have sounded slightly accusatory, but it's

weird. Usually nobody leaves until everyone is back at the shop.

He grabs the dust pan and holds it on the van floor. "The ladies do a weekly get together. I don't know what they do, but I know better than to interrupt their tradition. All the new guys went home, I guess. But I plan on hitting the bar as soon as we get locked up. Want to join?"

Do I? There's a small chance things could get awkward. Or, he could use this moment to confront me about his sister. Maybe we haven't been as secretive as she hoped. I'll be fine with everyone knowing, but I'm trying to keep my promise to Kate. Her pace is what's important to me, even if it's driving me bananas.

"Sure," I finish cleaning out the van, and lock it up, "is your girlfriend working tonight?"

"Yep. And if I'm lucky, she'll be able to sneak away from the kitchen for a bit."

"Are Wednesdays typically busy?"

Kai shrugs. "I don't actually know. I've never been on a Wednesday since it's not usually her day to work."

"I'll set the paperwork in the office, then I'll be ready to go."

"Sounds good."

I rush past Kai and put the delivery slips in a neat pile on the desk. Messy stacks are a pet peeve for Kai, and the last thing I want to do is piss him off since he's kind of my boss.

He's standing by the alarm when I return to the warehouse. "I'll meet you over there."

"Right behind you."

Realistically, I could walk. The bar isn't far from the shop. But I don't want to walk back when I'm ready to go home. Speaking of...

XANDER

> Hey, Mom. Going to the bar with a friend. I may be home later than usual.

MOM

> Okay. Have fun. ;)

What the hell? She must think I'm meeting a girl at the bar. It'd be preferred, but a guys' night sounds pretty great. It's much better than hanging out at home watching TV game shows with my parents.

I'm pulling out of the driveway when I see Kai walking to his car in my rearview. My stomach grumbles as I turn onto the road. It's a good thing they have food for a couple more hours.

The parking lot isn't as full as the last time I came, but there are a decent amount of people here. I find the closest spot I can to the door and head inside.

The first person I see is Mr. Jones, and I turn my back in hopes he doesn't see me. He's a nice man, but he likes to talk, and I don't want a redo of Valentine's night. I don't have an excuse of having to get back to work to cut him off.

The woman standing behind the stand smirks. I don't come here enough to know anyone by name, but she's totally laughing about my reaction.

"You saw nothing."

"I don't know what you're talking about." She glances at the top of her stand for a second. "Will you be heading to the dance area, or are you looking for a table?"

Good question. Kai said he wanted to eat, surely, he doesn't want to stand to do it. "Table, please. My buddy should be here soon."

The woman grabs two sets of utensils and menu before motioning for me to follow her.

"Hey, wait up," Kai calls from behind me, "I would have been here sooner, but I forgot to turn off a light and had to go back inside."

"Oh, hey Kai," the woman waves at him. "The table you usually get is open. Do you want that one?"

"That would be great, Delilah."

"You better be happy folks haven't really started showing up yet."

The both of us follow Delilah to a table on the far side of the room. It's pretty isolated. There's a small opening beside it that leads straight to the bar.

Once we're seated at the high top, Delilah sets the silverware and menus on the table. "Anthony will be here in a few to take your order. Enjoy."

"Thanks, Del." Kai gives her a salute.

"No problem." She waves and hurries back to the stand.

"What's so special about this table?" I pick up a menu and look it over before it's snatched out of my hands.

"You don't need that you're getting the wings," he

sets the menu on top of his untouched one. "This is the closest table to both the bar and kitchen. It's also sort of secluded, so I don't have to socialize if I don't feel like it."

"That sort of makes sense, but why do I have to get the wings?" It's not that I don't like them. I just like making my own eating choices.

"Because they are the best in the county and my girl-friend is making them."

It's cool Kai is supportive of his girlfriend but that doesn't mean he gets to tell me how to eat. "Can I see the menu please? I'm getting the wings, but I want to see what else there is."

He mumbles something under his breath and hands me a menu. A few moments later, a guy comes over and takes our order. He's back within minutes with our drinks.

Kai watches me for a few seconds. My stomach is in knots. What if this is all a ruse to accuse me of seeing his sister? I mean, it's a correct accusation. He doesn't know that, though. My hand tightens around my glass in the silence.

Finally, he speaks, "How is the job working out for you? Are you settling in, okay?"

My entire body relaxes, and I hope he doesn't see it. I don't need him asking more questions. "The job is great. Even though it's in the same realm of my previous job, delivering flowers is much better than pizzas. Seeing the pure joy these folks have when they get a delivery is pretty freaking amazing."

Kai rolls his eyes, "You sound like Emily. She's the romantic of the group."

"I've noticed." Our food arrives and I grab a wing to take a bite. "You better hope I don't regret this."

"You won't." Kai doesn't waste a second as he bites into the wings. He truly loves these things.

My teeth sink into the tangy meat, and he's not wrong. The flavor is amazing, and I don't think I've had wings that taste quite like this. There's just enough sauce covering them that it's flavorful, but not messy. I stop chewing when I notice Kai staring in the direction of the door.

"What are they doing here?" Kate, Emily, Sam, and Caroline just walked through the door. She can't answer a text, but she can come out? I knew she wanted to keep things low profile, but that still requires some sort of communication.

CHAPTER FIFTEEN

AS MUCH AS I love hanging out with my friends outside of work, this is not where I want to be right now. The bar is actually pretty slow right now. It's weird because the past few months have been full of holidays and it's been hard for us to get a table. Tonight, though... Delilah walks us straight to a high top in the middle of the room.

"Are we ever going to get a different table?" Samantha groans. "Caroline got the guy; she doesn't have to make eyes with him across the room anymore."

"Just because the rest of us are single doesn't mean we have to bash Caroline flirting with her other half."

"He's not my other half...yet," Caroline grins and stares at her ringless finger. "But I have a feeling our day is coming."

"I swear if you are a difficult bride, I'll throw you out of the shop." I grumble. The last bride I met with keeps changing her mind. We really need to update our contract on how many changes can happen throughout the process.

"In case you forgot, I have a key." She pulls her keys out of her pocket.

"Yeah, yeah," I wave her off, "I'm gonna get a drink."

Yes, they'll come take our order, but I need some space. Turning toward the bar, I stop in my tracks. My brother and Xander are sitting in a table in the furthest corner in the room, both of them focused on me. What in the hell are they doing here?

I dip between patrons and the waitstaff until I'm in front of them. "Kai? Why are you ruining my weekly night out with my friends?"

The shock on Xander's face hits me in the gut. I told him we'd go out tonight to make up for last night. I really tried to get out of it, but my friends kept insisting. It's not like they've never missed a night out. But I get it, there's been a lot going on with the shop and we all need to decompress.

"I don't know what you're talking about." My brother says before smirking and glancing at Xander. He knew exactly what he was doing.

I can't say something to him right now. Later, though, he'll be hearing everything I have to say. He purposefully brought Xander here tonight. Why? I don't know. But it seems we haven't been as secretive as we thought.

He taps on the top of the table before standing. "I need to hit the restroom. I'll be right back."

As soon as my brother vacates his seat, I slide into it.

Because he's an ass, I help myself to some of his fries. When I glance up, Xander's eyes are on me.

"I thought we were hanging out tonight." It's not a question, but an accusation. He's not wrong to be upset.

"I tried to. We have weekly friend dates. It's how we hang out outside of work and we're not allowed to talk about the shop. I did everything I could to get out of tonight, but they wouldn't have it. I'm so sorry."

"Honestly, I can understand that. But you could have texted me to let me know." I grab his beer and take a sip. "I'm not the type of guy to try and pull you away from your friends. It just would have been nice to know we weren't getting together. Then your brother invited me out, and I thought what the hell, only to see you walk in."

Damn. I really did hurt his feelings. This is completely new territory for me. Well, relationships in general are new to me. I've never had to live my life wondering how it's going to affect another person. "I really am sorry. My phone died and I didn't think to charge it until we were leaving the shop."

I know as soon as the words leave my mouth, it's not a good enough excuse. I wouldn't believe it if the shoe was on the other foot.

"I guess your brother brought me here on purpose?" Hurt flashes through his eyes, and I wish we were anywhere else but here.

"Most likely." I run my hands over my braid. It's a nervous habit I wish I could stop, but alas it's here to stay. "I think they may have all been in on it to see if they could confirm that we're seeing each other because my friends conveniently didn't have a charger I could use for my phone."

Xander glances in the direction of the table I left moments ago. "I'd say by the way they are staring in our direction, you're right."

"I guess the cat's out of the bag." I sigh and grab another fry off my brother's plate. "There were easier ways they could have asked."

"Or, we could have been upfront from the beginning." Xander stares at me, knowing he's right. This is all my doing because I was too scared to let my friends know that deep down, I might actually want a relationship.

"In hindsight, that may have been the best course of action." Even now I refuse to fully admit he was right all along. "So, what do we do now?"

"Well, it seems like they know, so we might as well stop hiding. It'll definitely make being at work easier."

"What do you mean?"

"Do you have any idea how hard it is to keep my eyes off you when we're in the same room? Or not being able to tell you bye, when we leave? It's torture."

Wow. I don't think I've ever met anyone who feels that deeply. Even the guys that pursued me in college and after only wanted to get in my pants more than I was willing to allow. But that's not all Xander wants. For whatever reason he actually wants *me*. My parents don't even make me feel that I'm wanted. Only that I'm tolerated because I'm their daughter. It's one of the reasons I never understood how Kai has managed to keep a somewhat positive relationship with them. He is the golden child, though.

"I didn't realize it was that hard." Another lie. It's been difficult for me as well.

"Please, I see the way your eyes linger just a tad too long and you glance around the room to make sure nobody else noticed. Even though it looks like they've seen everything," he reaches across the table and grabs my hand, "look, I don't give a damn what anyone else thinks. I want to be with you. I thought I could handle hiding things at work, but I can't. And now that everyone knows, we shouldn't have to. I'm not saying we need to be all over each other like my parents because honestly, that's a little much for even my tastes. Let's just go with the flow."

"I think I can do that." He titles his head and gives me a look. I'm not sure what that means. "It's what I can offer right now. Even though I'm a few years older than you, I don't have a ton of experience with relationships. I haven't actually been in one since high school, but I'll try."

"That's all I'm asking." He lifts my hand and kisses the top of my knuckles. It something out of a romance movie, but I can't deny the butterflies it sends fluttering in my stomach. This is something I can get used to.

Clapping erupts from across the room, louder than the music playing through the speakers, and we look for the source. Our co-workers, including my brother, are grinning as they make their applause. "It's about damn time," Kai yells and everyone's attention turns to us.

"Want to get out of here?" Xander nods toward the door.

"Absolutely." I can't keep the grin off my face. This is what it feels like to be happy, and unafraid of showing it.

Xander lets go of my hand, pulls out his wallet, and throws some bills on the table. Probably enough to cover his and my brother's meal because that's the type of guy he is.

"We can grab something to eat on the way to your place."

"Didn't you just eat?"

"Yeah, but I can't let you eat alone." Further proof he's genuinely a good guy. I'd honestly be a moron to let this slip through my fingers.

⁂

"Any luck finding an apartment?" We're sitting on the sofa with the TV going in the background, cartons from the local Chinese restaurant on the coffee table in front of us.

"I honestly haven't looked around much," Xander says as he takes a bite of his food. "Everything has been busy at the shop, and I want to make sure I have enough money saved up," another bite. "When I leave home, I don't want to go back. It needs to be for good."

"That's understandable," I take a sip of my wine, "I can help if you want me to. There are a few decent complexes around here. Or, I think Carlos may be looking to rent his out soon. With things going well between Eric and Joan, I'm sure they'll be looking for something bigger to accommodate their family."

"Where is that?" I forget he doesn't know everyone like I do. Or, well, maybe he does...just not in the same age range.

"It's actually not far from here. The neighborhood is nice, and it's about the same distance drive to the shop as it is from here." He should know that drive by heart. He's stayed over more than I've ever let anyone before. "It's a cute little house."

"I don't know if I'm ready for that kind of responsibility. Apartments are a safe transition for me. Not much different than living in dorms."

"Plus, the added benefit of not having others share a room full of showers."

The shock on his face is adorable. "Um, I didn't have to do that. I mean, I did, but it wasn't like what they show in those old movies."

Wow. Even ten years difference is a world apart between us, and I never felt that way until those words left his mouth. "Lucky you." I raise my glass in a toast to him.

"That's not what I mean, Kate."

"I know." Setting my glass on the table, I sigh. "It's jarring sometimes thinking about all the differences between us."

"Why don't you think about the things we have in common?"

"Which would be?"

He sets his food on the table and leans back. "The ability to make fun of infomercials."

"I think most people do that."

"Okay, how about the fact we both like cheesy sci-fi movies?"

"A new development for me. I never would have given them a chance if it wasn't for you."

"We both like to go out for a drink after a long day." He's reaching for things now.

"That's true."

"And we have the ability to talk without it feeling difficult. That's something I've never had with anyone else." He runs a hand through his dark brown hair. "Not even my friends in college sometimes. It's honestly a little ridiculous how much of a loner I was before I started working at the flower shop."

"You could have fooled me," I snort and pick up my glass, "you fit in with our group like you've always been there."

He blushes, before standing and gathering his food cartons. "It's, uh, getting late. I should probably get home."

I glance at my now charged phone. It's after midnight. "How does time pass so quickly when we hang out?"

"I don't know, but it definitely seems to fly by." He heads to the kitchen and I hear the fridge door open. It's sweet he's putting his leftovers in there for me. I wait for him to return to the living room before I say anything else.

"You could stay if you want." If he does, he might as well start leaving a change of clothes and toothbrush over here. Even though he's only stayed over a few times, I sleep better when he's next to me.

"As much as I'd love to, I better go home."

"Oh, okay." I try to keep the disappointment out of my voice, but he can clearly see it on my face.

"How about I pick you up for work in the morning?"

"That would be great."

He bends down and gives me a quick peck on the lips. I guess he knows if he lingers he won't be leaving for the night. "Goodnight, Kate. And don't make any plans this weekend. I'm cooking you dinner."

This I have to see; I don't think I've ever had anyone cook dinner for me.

xander

SCROLLING through my phone while waiting to load my next delivery probably isn't a good use of time, but I do want to get my own place. I'd be lying if I said the thought didn't scare me as much as it excites me.

Now I only need for these apartments to be within my price range. Most of them are higher than my parents' house payment. I may have peeked at a bill out of curiosity. Mostly to see if I could honestly afford to rent the house Carlos has if it goes up for rent.

"I thought you weren't seriously looking?" Kate leans over my shoulder.

There's no fear in her being close to me, or even leaning her head on me. Not now that everything is out in the open. Well, at least as far as our coworkers are concerned. We still haven't gone on an actual date. At least not one where we are in the public eye. That is something I hope to change very soon. We just have to figure out a time that works for both of us. Which is hard because it's getting into peak wedding season.

"I wasn't. Not really." I sigh and close the browser on my phone. "It's just I feel like I'll wear out my welcome always going to your place. It would be nice to invite you to mine."

Something I can't do as long as I live with my parents. Unless she wants to meet them. After our breakthrough, I don't want to suggest it, not yet.

"You can come over anytime, but I get it." She glances at the whiteboard at the far corner of the room. "About dinner this weekend...are you okay about doing it Sunday night?"

"Sure. Did something come up?"

"Caroline's son has some school thing and she asked me to fill in at a wedding for her. It shouldn't take too long, but I never know if something will go wrong." She plays with the end of her braided hair, waiting for my response. I've noticed that's something she does when she's unsure about something. It's cute.

"It's all good." I pause for a second as an idea hits me. "If you need help, I'm available. We don't have many deliveries queued up for Saturday as of right now."

"Are you sure?" I can't read her expression, and I'm having doubts about the offer. "You already do so much extra stuff around here. I don't want to monopolize your time off."

"Really. You'd be doing me a favor."

"How so?" She cocks her head to the side, waiting for my answer.

"It's my parents' anniversary, and the last place I want to be is home whenever they get back from whatever they have planned." My whole body shivers in revulsion.

Kate laughs so loudly, everyone looks in our direction. I don't think they've ever seen her this carefree with someone judging by their expressions. I'd be lying if I said it didn't make me feel good about myself. *I'm* the one capable of bringing the reaction out of her.

"Well, I'd be evil if I didn't save you from parental groping."

"Oh, God," I fake gag, "don't ever say those two words together again."

"I second that," Samantha calls from the work table, "it's disgusting and disturbing. Why would you even speak it into existence?"

"Please," Kate scoffs, "Your parents, and Emily's, were the same way."

"Exactly." A quick glance around Kate, and I can see Emily shake her head. "We've been scarred for life. I'm sure you feel our pain, Xander."

"I'm still living the nightmare, but yeah, I know exactly how you feel." It's not fun, even though I appreciate how much love they still have for each other.

"Okay, fine," Kate throws her hands in the air, "I'll stop making mushy parent jokes."

She smiles, but I can see how much she wanted that sort of upbringing in her eyes. There's a sadness just behind the sparkle and it affects everything she does.

"Xander," Kai yells from the hallway, "you've got a delivery."

I glance at my phone and groan. I'm almost afraid to ask. "Where is it?"

"The other side of Dallas."

Yep. I shouldn't have asked. At this time of day traffic is going to be horrible. Emily moves from the work table to the computer. "It's not too difficult. I'll have it ready in ten minutes."

"Thanks," I call out, "any chance you want to ride along with me?"

A small grin lifts the corner of Kate's mouth. "I wish I could, but I have to double check the order for the wedding this weekend. We're supposed to get the delivery in the morning."

"Fine," I grumble, "I'll face the traffic gods on my own."

"It's not that bad," she laughs and leans over to give me a quick kiss, "but if I'm gone before you get back, text me."

"I will." My fingers are crossed she'll be here and we can grab dinner. But I don't want to overstep. Spending too much time together outside of work may freak her out, and that's the last thing I want.

There's only one car in the lot when I get back to the shop. It's not Kai or Kate's. My heart sinks at not being able to see Kate before I go home, but I need to make sure I'm not overstepping her boundaries.

Emily is sitting at the work table with various flowers around her. "You're here late."

She jumps at the sound of my voice, and I feel bad for scaring her. It's not like the door is quiet when it's open or closed. She must have really been in the zone. "Just trying to finish the last of these arrangements for a wedding tomorrow night. Thank God it's not a huge number of flowers."

"The others didn't stay to help?" That feels pretty crappy in my opinion.

"Nope. I sent them home. Both Sam and Kate will be feeling the struggle tomorrow night, and their orders are much bigger. The plus side for Kate is Caroline will be here to help her."

"What about Sam?"

"I'm sure Caroline will help her, too. I'd be here, but my parents are having another mandatory dinner. You'd think I wouldn't have to go since I have work obligations, and I'm an only child. But it's the one thing they ask for. It's kind of hard to deny them that."

"I feel your pain," I run a hand through my hair. "My parents are way less strict than yours, though."

"Honestly, I think everyone's parents are cooler than mine. Except maybe Kate's." She grimaces as soon as the words leave her lips. As if she's said too much.

"What's the story there?"

"If she hasn't told you, I'm not sure it's my place,"

she points to some wire on the table against the wall, "can you hand me that?"

I grab it and bring it over to her. It should feel odd being alone with her, but it's not. It's almost like we're honorary siblings since we're both only children.

"She's mentioned some things. Well, mostly that she's not close to her parents. Not like Kai is."

"I wouldn't exactly call Kai close to them. He's just able to tolerate more since they think he's the best thing in the world. All the while, they give Kate crap over every little thing she does. I swear when I see the whole dynamic in person, it makes me grateful I'm an only child."

"Yeah, I don't think that's something I'd like to witness," I shake my head, "it does make me wonder if all families are like that. Well, ones with multiple children."

"No. Sam and her sister are treated exactly the same even though they are polar opposites."

"Is she grouchy, too?"

"Not even a little bit," Emily laughs, "it's a wonder they came from the same household."

"Well, I think it's great the four of you are as close as sisters. I don't think I've ever had a friend group that likes to hang out like y'all do. And the fact y'all have been friends since you were kids, is pretty incredible."

Emily shrugs as she rearranges the flowers she was working on. "We kind of did our own thing. We knew everyone in school, but were mostly concerned with ourselves. I'd like to say it kept us out of trouble, but that would be a lie. The other three tried to take the brunt of the punishment back then because of how strict my parents were."

"That's cool," I glance at the clock, "I should probably head home. If these weddings are as much work as Kate says, I'll need all the rest I can get."

"The one she's taking over shouldn't be too bad. It's a smaller wedding. But it's not a bad idea to get some rest."

"See you tomorrow," I wave before heading for the door, "be careful on your way home."

"You, too."

Despite learning some things about Kate, I am grateful I'm an only child. Even if it would have been fun to have a sibling to play with as a kid.

❋

"Y'all do this every time you have a wedding?" I'm helping Kate and Caroline with the arrangements for the wedding. Well, as much as I can anyway. Mostly, I'm grabbing the flowers they need and setting them on the table. As far as making them pretty, I'm no good at that.

"Yep," Kate glances at me before fixing another arrangement, "luckily, this isn't a massive wedding. We'd be preparing for it days before if that was the case."

"I guess I never realized how many flowers a wedding needs." I think back to all the romcoms my mom made me watch with her. "I thought it was just the bouquets and those little flower things the guy's wear."

"If you want a super simple wedding with little to no decoration," Caroline grins. "Which is totally fine. I actually prefer making arrangements for those. But these days everyone wants to have a ceremony that photographs well for social media."

"That's not really my thing." Thank God. I've scroll through social media, but I don't post very often.

"I didn't realize you were thinking about popping the question." This time Caroline laughs at the wide-eyed expression on Kate's face.

"Th-that's not what I meant. For the future, far future. I'm not looking to get hitched right now." I really hope that eases some of the fear I see across Kate's face. The last thing I need is her freaking out and thinking those thoughts have entered my mind.

"I know," Caroline bends over as she tries to contain her almost silent laugh. When she looks up, there are tears running down her face. "I wish the both of you could have seen the looks on your faces. You would have thought y'all were in a horror movie."

"You're such an ass." Kate picks up a fallen flower and throws it at her friend. "Do you like seeing how much you can torture me?"

"I mean," Caroline shrugs, "it's definitely fun. If you weren't so against love and commitment it wouldn't be this easy."

"Clearly I'm not that against it," Kate huffs and points at me, "last time I checked I'm dating Xander. Dating implies a commitment."

There's no way I'm jumping into this argument. It

won't lead anywhere good. It's between two friends. Even though they are talking about me like I'm not standing right here. Caroline does have a point. It felt like pulling teeth for Kate to admit she has any sort of attraction to me. She did not make it easy.

A few minutes pass and all you can hear is music playing softly over the speaker. Both of them are back in their workflow and it's like nothing happened. Maybe it's because they both have siblings. They know to let go of the small shit and keep forging ahead. I don't know, but the dynamic is something I've never seen before. At least not with anyone I went to college with, or even my friends in high school.

"What time do I need to be here tomorrow?" The sound of my voice startles both of them, and Kate drops one of the flowers in her hand. There isn't much for me to do, and while I'm enjoying the time with Kate, I feel kind of dumb just standing here in the background.

"Around eleven?"

"Sounds good," I point at the door behind me, "I think I'm going to head out."

"Oh, um, okay." I move toward her and give her a quick peck on the lips. I'm still not certain how she feels about full blown PDA in front of her friends. "I'll see you in the morning."

WATCHING Xander leave the shop last night bothered me more than I thought it would. Not because he was leaving, but because I wasn't leaving with him. It's something I've never felt toward someone before. As much as it scares me, the feeling also leaves me wanting to see him as much as I possibly can. Yeah, we work together, but the actual amount of time we're in the shop together isn't that much.

The door to the shop opens, and I know it's him before I even turn around. "Hey, are you sure you're up for this?"

"Absolutely," he wraps his arms around my waist, "as long as it means spending time with you, I'm ready for whatever you have to throw at me."

Little does he know how much work setup actually is. Kai normally helps out when we need an extra hand, but I'm happy Xander offered to be here today.

"You might regret that once we get there," I turn to face him, "you don't have to do this, you know."

"I do, but you need an extra set of hands, and I'm not doing anything. So, you should stop trying to get rid of me." He bends down and kisses along my jawline. A shiver rushes through me.

"I'm not," my voice is breathier than intended, "it's just this isn't actually part of your job description."

"Says who?" his voice is a soft whisper against my ear.

"Me?" I swear, he's going to be the death of me. All reason, and thought, flies right out the window when he's around me. It's not even sexual. Well, not all the time. It's him in general. How did someone like me attract a guy like him.

He leans back until his eyes meet mine. "You don't sound too sure about that."

"I-I am." I push him away to put space between us. If he keeps kissing me, we're not going to make it to the wedding. And that can't happen. Not now when we have all eyes on us. "You ready to help me load up everything?"

"Buzzkill," he mutters with a mischievous grin. He knows we have a job to do, so he doesn't push it. "Is it everything here on the table?"

"Yep," I point toward the shelf by the door, "and the basket over there has the bouquets and boutonnieres."

"That's what those things are called." He sounds way too excited about the revelation. "You have no idea how much that was bugging me last night."

I move toward the basket while he grabs a couple of the arrangements. "What did you end up doing when you went home?"

"Not much. Ate dinner with my parents so they'd leave me alone," he shrugs as he moves toward the door, "then played video games for a bit."

"Sounds like an exciting night."

"It could have been more exciting." He winks at me before opening the door and heading to the van.

It probably would have been had I not had to help Caroline with the last of the arrangements. She may have had a point about the whole commitment thing, but even though I want to spend my free time with Xander, I'm in no way ready to get hitched. It was cruel of her to even play around like that.

I follow him out the door with the basket in hand. "Are we still on for dinner tonight?"

"Absolutely," he turns after putting the flowers in the van. "We'll need to stop by the store when we're done, but I've got dinner completely figured out."

"What are you cooking?" I'm not much of a cook. He's probably noticed that from the lack of food in my fridge. I live off frozen dinners and takeout. The only thing that keeps me healthy is the amount of running around I do here at the shop, and the fact I walk to work as much as I can.

"That is a surprise."

"I'm not a huge fan of surprises."

"Why not?" He opens the shop door for me to follow him inside for the rest of the arrangements.

"One time I let my brother order pizza while he was staying on my sofa, and he ordered one with anchovies as a joke. I didn't find it very funny. It took forever to get the smell out of my apartment."

"Well," he laughs, "I can promise you there isn't fish involved in what I'm making. It's nothing fancy, just a quick recipe I learned from my mom."

Honestly, it's kind of a turn on that he knows how to cook, and he's willing to do it for me. "I can't wait to try it then."

"Speaking of..." he grabs another set of flowers and turns toward me, "I know this is really new for both of us, but how do you feel about coming to dinner tomorrow night?"

My mouth drops open. Meeting the parents is a big deal, or so I've been told. I'm not sure if I'm ready for that.

When I don't say anything, he backtracks. "You don't have to. It was just a suggestion. My mom wants to meet the person who keeps a smile on my face. It's not a big deal if you don't want to."

I grab some of the arrangements to busy my hands while I think of something to say. Dinner with his parents could be a breeze. They're nothing like my parents. It's something I'll need to remind myself of continually. Just because my parents suck, doesn't mean everyone else's does. Besides, it might be good to see how his parents interact. It'll give me more insight into Xander, and why he seems to be well adjusted.

"No, no it's fine." I turn toward him. His brows are

furrowed as he waits for my response. "The invitation was just unexpected. I would love to have dinner at your house. Do I need to bring anything?"

Take that Caroline. I can do the whole committed to one person thing. Even if it scares the shit out of me.

"Just yourself," he lets out a breath, relieved by my answer. "I was going to offer to pick you up, but figured you may want to drive over in case you felt the urge to get away as fast as possible."

Another way he's constantly thinking of me and my boundaries. "Honestly, it will be nice to see what it's like on the other side with parents who aren't completely self-absorbed and care about their kid's happiness."

That may have come out more bitter than I intended, but it doesn't make it any less true. I know he'll want to meet my parents eventually, but I plan on pushing that off for as long as possible.

Honestly, I'd be okay with him never meeting them. He knows all the important people in my life, and it doesn't include the people who birthed me.

"So, you'll come?"

How could I ever deny the hope in his voice? I'd have to be a monster. "Yes, I'll come."

Xander throws his hand in the air in victory. Small actions like that are what make me lo—. Hold up. It's not the "L" word. Lust, yes. Companionship, maybe. But love? Absolutely not. We haven't even known each other that long.

"My mom will be so excited." He grabs the last of the arrangements and heads to the van.

"Is there anything I should know before then? I don't want to offend them in any way."

He snorts and shakes his head. "I'm probably more worried about them offending you." He slides the arrangements into the van. "They like to joke around, but if anything they say makes you uncomfortable, just let them know and they'll stop. Or, tell me, and I'll say something."

"From what you've said about them, I doubt that will happen."

"It's not like they set out to offend people. They over-share and don't often think before speaking."

I watch him close the van doors before turning to lock up the shop.

"So, it'll be like hanging out with my brother."

Testing the handle before making his way to me and the van, he nods. "That's actually pretty accurate. Want me to drive?"

"That would actually be great." This is another one of those small things he does to make me appreciate him more.

***

Xander's arm flexes as he cooks the meat. We made it back from the wedding set up in record time. Luckily, the bride decided to keep all the arrangements so we don't have to go back to the venue to pick up anything.

Eyeing the ingredients on the counter, I can't quite figure out what it is he's making. A can of cream of mushroom soup, beans, and salsa are grouped together on the counter.

"What exactly are you making?"

He glances over at me and grins. "You'll see. You have to trust the process."

"I guess." I've never seen these ingredients go into one dish. Plus, there is a bag of tortilla chips he says we'll need.

"Do you have a strainer?"

Do I? "Let me look."

I bend down and rummage through the cabinets. Finally, I find it shoved in the back corner. I'm shocked I've had everything he's needed. I should probably learn to cook. It's never been high on my priority list.

I take it to the sink to wash and dry it. He drains the small amount of grease into a bowl then returns the meat to the pan. He opens the cans and adds them to the meat mixture. Then he adds a small amount of salsa. Turning the burner on, he mixes it all together.

I never thought watching someone cook would be attractive. But the level of confidence he has cooking this dish is a turn on.

As the meat simmers, he opens the bag of chips and covers the bottom of a baking dish. He presses on the chips slightly to break them up. Once that's done, he pours the meat mixture on top and covers it with shredded cheese. At least now I know it's some sort of casserole. From the amount of cheese he's put on top, it's a good thing I'm not lactose intolerant.

"How long does it take now?" I'm taking mental

notes on how to make it because this actually looks easy enough for me to do without screwing it up.

"Long enough for the cheese to melt." He takes the baking dish and slides it into the oven that has been preheating while he cooks. "It feels weird making such a small portion of it. When I was in college, my roommates and I had this at least once a month. I would have to triple or quadruple it to make enough to feed all of us. And there were never leftovers."

"Y'all cooked while you were in college?"

"Yep. A few of us knew our way around a kitchen and we'd take turns." He furrows his eyebrows in confusion, "you didn't?"

"Nope," I shake my head, "I'm sure I would have burned down the dormitory. I either got food from the cafeteria, or I'd use my tips to buy my meals. I wasn't lying when I said I wasn't much of a cook."

"I guess I'll have to teach you, then."

"Are they all as easy as this?" If so, I'll have a much easier time preparing meals.

"For the most part. There are other more elaborate meals I know how to make, but I don't do it often because it takes too much time. Plus, my mom usually handles dinner unless my dad decides to grill."

"Understandable. It must have been nice to have parents who taught you how to do the most basic things to survive. My mom tried to teach me how to cook exactly one time."

"It didn't go well?"

"Not in the slightest." I glance toward the stove

remembering how horribly it went. "She got frustrated with me because I put a tad too much of one ingredient and claimed it would mess up the entire recipe. After that, she pretty much banished me from the kitchen."

"That's kind of sad," he turns on the oven light and bends down to check the progress of the cheese before standing again. "But, so you know, on most dishes, you don't have to worry about adding a little extra. My mom doesn't measure anything when she cooks. She seasons until it feels right."

"That sounds like magic."

"It is in a way," he grabs a hand towel, opens the over, and pulls out the dish. "Mom says once you've had practice, it's easier to know when to stop," he slides the dish on top of the stove, "and, now, dinner is served."

I pull a couple of plates out of a cabinet and grab silverware from the drawer, setting them on the counter next to the stove. "It smells amazing."

Xander grabs a plate and adds some of the casserole to it. Then does the same to the other. "If you like a little kick, add some hot sauce."

"I think I'm good." Spicy isn't something I'm a fan of, unlike most of my friends. "I wish I had a small table in here for us to eat at, but we'll have to use the coffee table."

"It's fine." He grabs the bottle of hot sauce he bought and shoves it in his pocket before picking up both plates and carrying them into the living room.

The only drinks I have are bottled water and wine.

I'm not sure what to pair with this, so I grab a couple of waters and follow after him.

There's music playing softly from his phone on the table and he's waiting until I join him before lifting a fork. "Sorry, I don't have anything else."

"You're good," he smiles at me as I set the waters down and join him on the sofa, "now, take a bite and tell me what you think."

It's unnerving having him watch me eat, but he went through the effort of making me a meal, and I'll give him this small satisfaction. I scoop a bite of the casserole, making sure to get a little of each layer before lifting it to my mouth.

As much as I questioned the combination of ingredients, they work well together. The chips add a slight texture difference and it tastes like home. Not my home obviously, but what it felt like when I had dinner with my friends. Also, it's weird to describe food as home, but I have no other way to word what it tastes like.

"It's delicious," I say after I swallow my bite, "really, it's not like anything I expected."

"Whew, I'm glad you like it." The pride he feels in making something for me lights up his face. It's in this moment I know I'm screwed because maybe, just maybe, love is what I'm starting to feel toward him.

xander

DINNER LAST NIGHT WAS A SUCCESS. I can only hope tonight is just as successful. She texted me earlier letting me know she's still coming. Nerves shoot through my body about Kate meeting my parents.

When I made the offer yesterday, I thought she was going to turn me down. Her wide eyes didn't give me much hope that she'd say yes. I do wonder if the conversation she had with Caroline the other night is part of the reason. Maybe she feels the need to prove her friend wrong. Either way, I'm officially freaking out now.

"Xander," my mom yells from somewhere else in the house. She probably wants to ask about Kate, or get me to do something else around the house. Since I told her she was coming for dinner, she's been in cleaning mode. Everything has to be perfect, or as close to, in her eyes before first time guests come over. After that, the guest is family and she doesn't go overboard.

I double check my hair in the mirror before walking

out of my room and closing the door behind me. Now to find my mom. It's not a big house, but her voice carries and she could be anywhere.

She's in the living room with a duster in hand. "You called me?"

Mom jumps at the sound of my voice. "Oh, I didn't think you'd come so quickly. It usually takes you ages to answer me."

Shrugging, I glance around the room. Did she move the furniture? "Being in my room and getting anxious about Kate coming over wasn't helping matters. Do you need me to do something?"

"I need you to sweep and mop the kitchen."

"Didn't you do that this morning?" I honestly believe there is such a thing as over cleaning.

"Yes," she sighs, "but your father was mowing and tracked grass all over the place."

"Anything else you need me to do?" She keeps tapping the end of the duster on the shelf and I know her nerves are as high as mine are. They may actually be higher.

"Do you think we should order in instead of cooking? I don't want her to hate what I'm making."

"Absolutely not," I shake my head so she gets the memo. "All Kate does is eat out. It'll be nice for her to have a home cooked meal, and I think she'll appreciate the effort."

"If you say so. Now go get that done, and then we're okay for the most part." She turns back to dusting before pausing. "And we'll try to be less touchy feely in front of y'all tonight."

"It's fine, Mom." I love that she's worried about that, but it's not necessary. "After what she's told me about her parents, the fact that y'all still show your love grosses me out less."

"You probably shouldn't have told me that." She winks and returns to dusting. Why does it feel like I gave them the go ahead to make things as embarrassing as possible for me?

⁂

The doorbell rings and my mom rushes around the living room. She's fluffing the pillows again and doing one last glance to make sure nothing is out of place. I don't know why. I mean, I do, but Kate knows how much time we spend in the living room.

"Can I answer the door now?" The fear of Kate leaving if I don't answer right away is spiking.

"Yes, yes. Go ahead." She shoos me toward the door before standing still with her hands in front of her. Dad is sitting in the recliner and she scowls at him. "Get up Edward. You can't be sitting when she comes in."

Groaning dad gets up and stands beside her as I'm making my way toward the door. A quick look back has me shaking my head. They look like that painting of the farmers with their pitchforks. Faces devoid of emotion, and focused ahead. So much for them not being weird. I hope Kate's ready for this.

"You made it," I say before the door is even all the way open. Her eyes are on her shoes. She has a bottle of wine in one hand and flowers in the other.

"Am I early?"

"Not at all," I grin at the flowers, "you know, it's customary for me to give you flowers, not the other way around."

"They aren't for you," she rolls her eyes, "they are for your mom. And the wine is for everyone. One thing my parents drilled into my head is you don't show up somewhere empty handed."

"I think it's a dumb rule, but it's appreciated." Opening the door wider, I wait for her to take a step inside. She doesn't move. "Are you going to stand on the porch all evening?"

"Oh, sorry." Finally, she moves one foot over the threshold. I take the bottle of wine from her, and usher her further inside so I can close the door.

"Mom, Dad, this is Kate," I hold up the bottle I took from her, "she brought wine."

"These are for you, Mrs. Charles." Kate holds the flowers out for my mom. "I wasn't sure which flowers would suit you, so I grabbed a few colorful ones. From what Xander has said about you, I think these fit in perfectly."

"Oh, thank you, Kate," Mom takes the flowers and smells them, "they smell divine, and they are beautiful."

"If you bring her flowers every time you come over, I'm gonna have to up my game." Dad chuckles as he wraps his arm around Mom's shoulder and kisses her on top of the head. Yeah, Mom definitely took it as a challenge and told Dad.

"Well, you know where to come to get them. And, you'll get the family and friend's discount." She winks at him at my parents, and it's adorable. So far so good. It looks like meeting my parents won't be a complete disaster for either of us.

"I'm going to put these in a vase and get dinner started." Mom turns toward the kitchen.

Before she can take too many steps, Kate speaks up again. "Do you need any help?"

"Honey, you don't have to help me cook. You're a guest."

"I'd like to, though. Cooking isn't my strongest suit, and I'd love to join you, even if it's only watching you."

"There isn't much to cooking spaghetti, but you can come see what I add to it."

"Thank you." Kate glances up at me with a small smile and follows my mom into the kitchen.

A part of me wants to follow them. To make sure Mom doesn't say or do anything that's going to upset Kate. She hasn't exactly had the best parents from what she's told me. I don't want my parents to add to that parental stress she carries around with her.

"Sit down, son," Dad's voice is gruff as he makes his way to his recliner. "She'll be fine. Your mother isn't a monster."

"I know," I run a hand through my hair and take a seat on the couch while he flips through the channels to find something to watch. "She doesn't have a relationship with her parents like the one we have. I worry is all."

"Xan, she's a grown woman who owns her own business. I'm pretty sure she can take care of herself." He settles on an action film since Mom isn't in here. Otherwise, it would be another romcom we've seen a million times. "Besides, this will be good for her and your mom."

"You're right." If I keep repeating it to myself maybe it'll make it true. "What do you think about her?"

His opinion is something I want. Not that it'll change my mind on anything regarding Kate, but I need to know if they'll clash.

"I like her. The wine wasn't necessary, but she brought flowers for your mom. Anyone who shows your mother what a treasure she truly is, is golden in my book."

"Gee, thanks. You don't care about how she treats me?"

"That's not what I'm saying, kiddo." Ugh, I hate when he calls me that. As if I'm not in my twenties and doing my best to get my shit together. "If she treated you badly, you wouldn't be with her. You would never have brought her home to meet us. This is the first woman you've brought home to meet us since you were in high school. There's a reason for that, and I trust your judgement when it comes to your heart. When you know, you know."

This is the first time I think we've ever had a conversation about my relationships since I was a teenager. He's not wrong, though. Maybe that's why I left my number that first night. There's something about Kate that pulls me to her.

Laughter floats into the living room from the kitchen. Dad and I are still watching the movie, but it's good to know my mom and girlfriend are getting along. Earlier Dad mentioned the girl from high school, but Mom couldn't stand her. Not that I blame her. It's not the she was a bad person, but she was very selfish and didn't treat me the best. It took a long time for me to realize it, and both of my parents were happy when things didn't work out between us.

There are times being high school sweethearts works out, but I'm grateful that wasn't the case for me. I never would have gone off to college or met Kate.

The movie credits are rolling when Mom calls out, "Dinner is ready."

"Do you have any idea what she was making?" I ask Dad. "Dinner never takes this long."

"I thought it was spaghetti," he shrugs as he stands from the recliner, "maybe she changed her mind."

We make our way to the kitchen and dad was right, she made spaghetti. But now there are brownies cooling on the counter. "So, Kate needs to come over for you to make brownies?"

"No, Xander," Mom shakes her head, "she asked me to teach her to make them. So, I did."

"You realize you'll need more in your fridge than the

bare necessities to cook, right?" I smirk in Kate's direction.

"After that comment, I may never cook," Kate sticks her tongue out at me. "You'll have to get used to cooking for me forever."

I can see the second she realizes what she said. Her eyes widen and she sputters, "Or, however long we're together. Not that I'm putting an expiration date on us. Oh my God." She buries her head in her hands.

"Don't worry," I move to her side and wrap an arm around her waist, "I'll cook for you as long as you'll have me."

Dad winks at me and smiles knowing damn well I mean it. I pull out the chair next to mine and wait for Kate to take a seat. Mom and Dad both sit in their usual spots. Mom motions for everyone to fill their plates and I don't wait for another suggestion. I've barely eaten today in anticipation of Kate coming over.

She nudges me in my side after I take my first bite. "So, how does it taste?" Her voice is barely above a whisper and it takes me a moment to realize why she's asking.

"It's great." I mutter around my mouthful of spaghetti.

"Kate helped season the sauce and meat," Mom beams, "I told her it was perfect, but she wouldn't hear it from anyone but you."

"Are you sure?" Kate asks again. "It's not too herb-y?"

"Not at all," I take her hand in mine, "I told you; your heart and intuition tell you when to stop."

"Ah, he does listen when I teach him to cook," Mom laughs before taking a bite. "His grandma taught me the same way. I don't even know if she had measuring cups. She always knew when the ingredients were just right."

"That's not how my mom cooks at all," Kate shakes her head, "everything has a precise measurement."

"To each their own." That's what Mom says, but I have a feeling she's already formed an opinion about Kate's parents, and I hope that doesn't get in the way of anything if, and when, they meet each other.

"For what it's worth, I think I like the way you cook." Kate's smile is small. I wonder if she's thinking about how things could have been different for her if her parents were more like mine.

"Thanks, but all the credit on this dinner goes to you."

"She's not wrong," Dad says, "this is really good."

"Thank you, Mr. Charles." She takes a bite of her own food, and from the soft moan that escapes her lips, I know she's proud of the meal she's helped make.

"Who's up for board games after we finish dinner?" Mom asks us.

"I don't know if that's such a great idea." It's a terrible one. We're incredibly competitive and there's nothing good that can come from that.

"Why not?" Kate pokes me in the side, "scared to get beat?"

Dad's laugh fills the room. "Oh, you're gonna fit right in."

I DON'T KNOW why I was so worried about meeting Xander's parents. They are polar opposites of mine. Their home feels cozy and lived in. A contrast to the magazine ready home I grew up in. Board games was never something we did as a family either. The only time I played them is with Kai or when I went to my friend's house.

Jealousy over the childhood I'm sure Xander had rears up. I'm not sure why other than the fact I had a wonderful time with him and his family. I wish I had that when I was a kid. Maybe my relationship with my parents would have been different.

The problem bride from a few weeks ago is due to be here in the next twenty minutes. Now is not the time to be thinking about all the things I missed in my childhood with my own parents.

"Hey, Sis," Kai approaches me in the warehouse, "I heard you met Xander's parents."

"Yep. It went shockingly well." What is going on with him? He doesn't usually ask about any of my personal life. "I even learned how to make brownies."

"That's impressive. So, when are you going to make some for your favorite brother?"

"You're my only brother." One day he'll realize that saying gets old. "And I haven't made them on my own yet. I want to try them myself before I possibly make someone sick with my baking."

"That seems like a solid plan." He glances at his phone to check the time. He knows I have a meeting soon, and he'll have to give up the office. "So, when are you going to introduce Mom and Dad to him?"

Woah. What the hell? The question throws me off, and it takes me a few moments to even garner a response.

"I don't see how that's any of your business."

"Because you've met his parents. If it's that serious, Mom and Dad should meet him." He puts his hands on his waist as if he's scolding a child. Too bad I'm older than him.

"You honestly think that will go over well? As if they don't judge every little thing I do."

"They aren't that bad."

"To you they aren't." God, how can he not notice how much they are on my ass and everything he does is brilliant? It's like we grew up in two separate households instead of under the same roof. "They comment on everything I do. It doesn't matter if it's a good thing or not, they always have criticism."

"Maybe it's your attitude toward them." He groans as soon as the words are out of his mouth. He knows he's said the wrong thing, and it's about to turn ugly.

The chair rolls backward, and falls over behind me as I stand. There's no holding back the rage roiling through my body.

"My attitude toward them didn't come until much later. They have always been harder on me, and expected more out of me. Hell, just three months ago you were sleeping on my couch to avoid staying with them. So don't get on your high horse and tell me my feelings are invalid." It takes everything in me not to yell, but we're at work and I don't need to let possible customers know about my personal business.

He holds his hands up in surrender, as if I might leap across the room and attack him. "I-I shouldn't have said that. I'm sorry." He watches me for a few seconds to see how I'm going to react. "But would it be terrible if you tried to fix your relationship with them? I'm not saying act like nothing ever happened to fracture your relationship, but be cordial to each other at the very least."

"That's a hard ask, little brother. It's not like if I talk to them everything will be sunshine and rainbows. They have to bend as well."

"Just think about it," he glances at his watch again, "you should probably head in there and get ready for your meeting."

"You're lucky I'm not canceling it." He doesn't seem to appreciate my glare as I make my way past him toward the office. "Do me a favor and butt out of my relationship. It doesn't concern you, and if I want to Xander to meet our parents I'll make it happen. Also, be happy we're pretty much the only ones here. The girls wouldn't have let you come at me with that."

"I'm sorry, Kate." His voice is flat. He knows just how badly he's screwed up in my eyes. I don't mind his mostly normal relationship with the parents. But he doesn't need to force that on me. It's my choice the relationship I have with them. I just hope he hasn't let it slip that I'm seeing someone.

"So, did your fickle bride make actual choices today?" Xander hands me my food from the bag. I'll try to cook one day, but after everything with my brother and the pain in the ass bride, I didn't have it in me.

"To my surprise, she did," I glance through my notes on the coffee table. "None of it matches and the flowers don't even go together, but it's progress. She made decisions and I'll abide by them if only to avoid another stressful meeting."

"Progress is progress." He grins as he pulls out his food from the bag. He studies my face for a few minutes. "Is everything okay? You seem tense."

He was making deliveries when my brother bombarded with his opinion, and I haven't told him what all was said. A part of me wants to vent about it all. The other part wants to keep it shoved inside because he won't understand how I feel. He has supportive parents, and gets along with them. There's no way in hell he can know what it's like to be under my parents' scrutiny.

"Yeah. It was...a long day." Nope, not ready to unload all my family disfunction on him just yet. He knows the basics and for now that's all he needs to know.

"Anything I can help with?"

The amount of care he constantly shows me is a stark contrast to what my own family does. I'd be perfectly fine with him never meeting Mom and Dad. It might be the only thing that keeps us inside our bubble of contentment. Even though I know it won't stay like this forever. Or, at least I don't think it will. Every couple gets out of that super happy phase, don't they?

"I wish." And I do. I wish all of this was easy. "But I'll figure it out. For now, I'll be happy the latest bride has settled on what she wants and count the victory."

"Sounds like a win to me," he picks up the remote off the table, "wanna watch more cheesy sci-fi?"

"Not until after we eat. Some of those scenes are gruesome." Even though the last one we watched wasn't exactly cheesy, I almost spit my food out a couple of times. Some of these movies are just shy of being categorized horror.

"I can deal with that." He takes a bite of his burger and sits for a second. "I think I may have found an apartment."

"Oh, yeah? Where?"

I don't miss the way he bites his lower lip, nervous over what I might think.

"In this complex, actually. Not in your building or

anything, but on the other side. Someone is moving out, and I'm high on the list of possible renters."

"That's great." I set my food down and give him a hug. "You'll finally have your own space."

"Don't get too excited. It's not mine yet," he pulls away from me. "I wasn't sure how you'd react to me being in the same complex. It wasn't on purpose. I think I joined the waitlist to at least ten apartments."

"We don't even have that many complexes in Asheville."

"I know. I looked in surrounding towns, too. I wanted to give myself options."

Honestly, he could move in here. It's not like we'd need another room. But I'm not ready for that. Not even close. Hell, we haven't even said the "L" word, yet. Even though with each day that passes, I think I'm falling.

"That's smart," I take a bite of my food, "did you ever talk to Carlos? I'm pretty sure Eric and his girlfriend are looking for another place. That house isn't big enough for them and two teenagers."

"No. I didn't want to say I'm looking and rush the process."

"This town is growing," I place my hand on his and squeeze, "you need to let Carlos know you're interested. If not, some other renter is going to swoop in and take that prime real estate. Besides, you'd pay as much rent there as you would an apartment. And the house has an actual yard."

He chuckles. "Why haven't you talked to Carlos about it?"

"I don't like doing all the maintenance stuff that comes with living in an actual house. Neighbors would be calling to complain about the grass because I live at the shop."

"Clearly, that's not entirely true."

"What do you mean?"

He points his finger between me and him, then twirls it to encompass the room. "Because we are both here and not at the shop. And I don't think you're there as much as you think you are."

He has a point. It all boils down to him. Before Xander danced his way into my life, I was always at the shop. Well, except for when we have girl's night. We also have more help now than we did back then.

"You're right."

"I have my moments," he smirks, "now hurry and finish eating so we can get this movie started."

"Why are you in such a rush?"

"Because as I hate driving home late from here. Do you have an idea how many cops are out waiting for someone to screw up in the middle of the night?"

"Um, not really," I take a sip of my soda, "you don't have to leave. You know that, right? I hope I haven't made you feel otherwise."

"Oh, no," he waves his hands in the air. "I know that. Leaving is my choice. We see each other at work, and usually grab dinner. I figured you must be getting tired of seeing me. I don't want to overstay my welcome when you need some alone time."

"Why do you think you're overstaying?"

"You said you don't do relationships, right? At least," he grins, "not until me. I'm worried that if we hung out too much, you'd get tired of me and what we have together. The last thing I want is to ruin what is a good thing."

His admission sends a stab of pain to my gut. I didn't realize he does that for me. Or that I've made him feel he has to do that. Does that make me a shitty human? No. It makes me someone who guards my heart with a fortress. It takes work to penetrate it. Somehow, Xander is chipping away at the stone without me even realizing it.

"You aren't ruining a good thing," I set my burger down on the wrapper and scoot closer to him. "I want you here whenever you want to be here. Believe it or not, it's getting harder to fall asleep without you by my side."

"So, you need someone to snuggle with?"

I didn't used to. It was difficult to fall asleep with someone next to me, and rush home as soon as possible. "Yeah, I think I do."

CHAPTER TWENTY

xander

KATE IS STILL ASLEEP. The contrast between how she acted when we first started seeing each other and now is night and day. It hasn't been that long, but she's more comfortable with me now.

That first night, she stayed firmly on her side of the bed. Last night, her arm and leg were wrapped around my body. Maybe it was her subconscious telling her not to let me go. Who knows. I'm not complaining, though. When I first saw her, I thought she was out of my league. Now, though, I can't imagine my world without her.

Love has almost slipped out of my mouth more times than I can count. After what she said last night, I might tell her exactly how I feel. Fear is the only thing holding me back. The four-letter word could derail our entire relationship, and that's the last thing I want.

Kate mumbles something in her sleep, and I slide out from under the comforter as slowly as possible. Yesterday seemed like a rough day, and I want to let her sleep as much as possible. There was something bothering her, and I know it was more than the bride she was working with. I only hope she'll tell me what it was at some point. Deep down, I have a feeling it had something to do with me.

I tiptoe out of her room and straight toward the kitchen. I get the coffee brewing and turn to the fridge. If luck is on my side, there will be food inside. Opening the door, I close my eyes so I don't have to see the bare shelves. They aren't, though. All of the staples most people keep in the fridge are in there.

Grabbing the carton of eggs, butter, and bacon, I feel pride in the fact she's feeling more comfortable with cooking. She must be who my mom is texting all the time. Most guys would freak out. Not me. I'm happy they get along. If they didn't, I'm not sure I'd be able to handle that. We're close knit, and it wouldn't bode well for our future if she didn't like Mom.

The bacon sizzles as I put it in the pan. This is going to wake her up, but at least it will be to the scent of yummy food. If I could, I'd wake her like this every morning. She deserves it after some of the people she has to deal with.

"Why are you awake?" her sleep laced voice comes from the edge of the hallway.

"Because we have work today and my body was ready to wake up." Since starting at the shop, I haven't been able to sleep in. It's like I have a natural alarm clock now. When I was delivering pizzas, I did most of that at night and would sleep in. Now it's the opposite, and I enjoy having my evenings free.

"Right." She moves toward me and wraps her arms around my waist, her face rests on my back. "One of the days I might actually call in to work. I don't remember the last time I had a vacation day."

"You wouldn't know what to do with yourself. You may complain about some of your clients, but you love what you do."

The bacon pops and hits her arm. "Ow. Cooking bacon should not be dangerous."

"All good things are worth a little pain." Not just bacon, but relationships, too. There will always be growing pains, but in the end, everything turns out okay.

"How philosophical of you," she laughs and moves away from me, "I'm gonna get ready if you don't need any help in here."

"I'm good. But I'll have to head home after we eat so I can get changed for work." At this point, I need to leave a bag of extra clothes in my car since I never know if I'll be staying over or not. "Not too sure how folks at work will handle me showing up in the same clothes as yesterday."

"They'll get over it."

"Or cheer for us. I swear, I think they are more invested in our relationship than we are."

"They want me happy." I glance behind me to see what she's doing, and the smile on her face makes her glow. "For the first time in a long time, I actually am."

"I'll do my best to keep it that way." It's the one thing I can say with complete confidence. Even though it's been a short amount of time, there's nothing I wouldn't do for this woman. Making her happy is my goal for as long as she'll have me. If I play my cards right, maybe that will be forever.

⁂

"I think you get here later and later every day." Kai laughs as I walk through the door.

"Nah, not every day." He's not wrong, I do push the time a little when I stay with Kate, but I feel like that's not really something he'd want to know. "Besides, I show up with food."

I hold the box of donuts in front of him. "Which is why I don't say anything." He places the box on the work table and glances around. "Is there enough for Paula? Last time she didn't get any and I felt bad."

"Yes, there's plenty." After that incident, I started adding another half dozen. "What do I have on the docket for today?"

"It's actually not too bad." Kai pulls his phone out of his pocket. He scrolls for a minute. "There aren't any holidays right now so orders are slowing down some. They'll pick up again once we get close to Mother's Day. Of course, we're going to need you to work more weekends soon."

"Wedding season?" Before working here, I never would have known that's a thing.

"Yep." Kai double checks his phone. "This will be my first one working here, but I already know it's going to be a doozy. Between Spencer's wedding and all the new clients they've had the past few months, we'll be lucky to have a weekend off."

"That's fine with me. More hours means a better apartment."

"Oh, you're still looking for one?" He seems confused as to why I'd say that.

"Yeah. I've found some in my price range, but they aren't that great. There's one I'm on the short list for, but it's not guaranteed. Also, the rent is higher than I want to spend." I didn't tell Kate all that. It's one thing she doesn't need to worry about.

"Oh, no," Kai shakes his head, "I assumed you'd already moved in with my sister since you're over there so much."

"She's not ready for that. I'm going at the pace she sets."

"Smart move." He glances around. Why do I have a feeling whatever he's about to say, he doesn't want other ears to overhear it? "Look, I know Kate met your parents, and I th—"

He doesn't get to finish whatever he was about to say because Kate walks in and stands beside me. "You think what?"

"I think it's awesome you met his parents." Kai runs a hand through is hair and chews on his lip. That's not what he was going to say, and I know he's feeling some sort of guilt.

"I do, too." She glares at him. There's no way I'm getting in the middle of whatever fight they are having. I don't have siblings, but from what I've heard disagreements can be intense.

Kai shoves his phone in his pocket. "I'm gonna go grab your delivery tickets."

"Thanks, man. Make sure to leave some donuts for Paula." Once he leaves, I turn toward Kate. "What was that about?"

Her focus is on anything but me. Whatever they are arguing about, she doesn't want to tell me. Which means...it has something to do with me. I grab her hand to get her attention.

"Fine," she mutters, "Kai thinks because I met your parents, you need to meet ours. He said it's unfair and that I need to grow up."

"Why don't you want me to meet them?" It doesn't take much guess work, but I'll give her a chance to voice her thoughts.

"Because I don't have the best relationship with them." She ticks off one finger. "Because everything I do, they have to criticize. And our age difference will give them something to harp on me about for ages."

I could not imagine having that sort of animosity toward my parents. They get on my nerves but they always have my best interests at heart and show it in loving ways. Come to think of it, I don't think they've ever criticized anything I want to do. If anything, they've encouraged me, but were there to catch me if things didn't pan out.

"If that's what you want, then I won't pressure you to meet them." Now, I know how Kai was going to finish that sentence, and I wish he wouldn't interfere. Not everyone has the same relationship with their parents within a household. "What happens between us, and who you share it with, is our business...nobody else's."

"Thank you."

"For what?" I notice Kai watching us from the hallway.

"Letting me make up my own mind about us and my parents. For now, I want to keep everything as separate as possible. I hope that will change one day, but right now...I don't see it happening."

Leaning forward I give her a quick peck on the forehead. I've learned minimal PDA at work is okay with her. "I better get to my deliveries. If not, you'll have angry customers."

"Yeah, I need to get ready for our meeting in a few hours."

I didn't know she had a meeting. She just had one yesterday. "With the same bride?"

"Nope," she laughs, "this time it's with the ones who started this whole circus. They are in town to visit Stella and Johnny, and wanted to meet with us."

"Count me out of that meeting." I hold my hands in the air.

"They are pretty great, so I'm not too worried about it. They just want to go over a few things and ask us about some recommendations."

"Have fun with that." After a brief wave, I turn toward the hallway. Kai tries to stop me when I get the delivery papers, but that's not going to work. He's not going to put me in between his sister's wishes and his. It's not fair to me. Right now, my only focus is doing my job, and making sure Kate is as stress free as possible.

Shockingly, almost everyone is still at the shop when I get back. It rarely happens so I'm happy I won't have to shut the shop down by myself. It's not that it's hard, it's the back half of the shop. When it's dark right before you walk out, it's creepy. Not as much now that it's not getting dark early like it did when I started working here. But still I don't like to be left alone if I can help it.

"Hey," Emily waves at me, "any chance you want to do another delivery?"

My eyes widen in horror. It's almost closing time, there's no way in hell I want to go back out.

Before I have a chance to respond, she busts out laughing. I'm talking bent over at the waist and can't catch her breath.

"Ignore her," Samantha grumbles, "she thinks she's a comedian."

"So, there isn't another order to take?"

"No," Sam shakes her head. Clearly, she's over Emily's shenanigans. "There isn't another order."

"Thank goodness." I glance around the room. Both Kate and Caroline are nowhere to be seen. "Where's everyone else?"

"Kai and Caroline went home. Kate's upfront helping

Paula," Emily says through deep breaths. That's what she gets for trying to give me a mini heart attack.

"Okay. Well, I'll see y'all in a bit."

I make my way through the hall and Paula passes me. "I'll see you tomorrow."

"You done for the day?"

"Yep. Kate said to go home. She'll get the front closed down."

"Cool. See you tomorrow." Before she gets too far, I ask, "Did you get donuts this morning?"

"Oh my gosh, yes!" She pauses, "thank you for getting extra. I don't think Kai realizes how many he eats as he's passing back and forth through the shop."

"I don't think he does, either."

"I'm gonna go now. Bye." She continues walking down the hallway. I think she's excited to be getting out a few minutes early.

It's only a few more steps until I'm in the store area. Kate is wiping down the counters, but the open sign is still flashing because there's still about ten minutes left until we actually close.

"Hey," I wrap my arm around her waist, "why are you closing up?"

"Paula looked flustered when I got back from my meeting. It seemed mean to keep her here when she didn't have to be." She sets the cloth down on the counter and turns until she's facing me. "I didn't think you'd be back so soon."

"I didn't either," I chuckle and lean my head against hers, "the traffic gods were on my side today."

"That's good. No traffic is always a good thing," she wraps her arms around my neck, "want to grab dinner somewhere?"

"Sure. What are you thinking?"

"It doesn't matter as long as I'm with you." She leans up to give me a kiss since nobody else is in here.

"Do you really think that's appropriate, young lady?" A stern voice breaks us apart. "Making out while at work isn't very professional."

"Shit," Kate whispers. Her cheeks are bright red, but I see the anger flash through her eyes.

CHAPTER TWENTY-ONE

YOU HAVE GOT to be kidding me. There's no way this is a coincidence. What are the odds the day Kai tries to get Xander into meeting my parents that my dad walks through the door? And why the hell didn't the bell above the door ring?

"D-dad, what are you doing here?" Turning, I extricate myself from Xander's hold and face him. I hate that my voice breaks when I speak to him. It makes me feel weak.

"I came to get flowers for your mother. Tomorrow is her birthday, remember?" Of course, I remember. Despite what they may think of me, I'm not a total screw up. "I didn't expect to walk in and find you with your tongue down this young man's throat." he pauses for a beat, "how old are you, anyway?"

Xander stiffens behind me, and I know he's about to say something. But I stop him before he can. "Xan, you should probably go."

"I ca—"

He doesn't get to finish. "I said go, Xander."

I turn just enough to see the hurt flash across his face. I didn't mean to raise my voice at him, but he doesn't need to be here to witness whatever is about to go down with me and my dad. He glances at me one more time before heading down the hallway and out of sight.

Moving around the counter, I hurry to the door and turn off the sign. It's not quite closing time, yet, but nobody needs to be a witness to this.

"Why are you here, Dad?"

"Getting flowers for your mother." His tone is matter of fact and brooks no room for argument.

"I would believe that if it was something you did on a constant basis. I've had this shop for a decade, and not once have you come in here to get flowers for her," I put my hands on my hips, "so, I'll ask you again why you're really here."

"I don't feel the need to explain myself to you." He crosses his arms over his chest.

"Then you can leave." I open the shop door and hold it for him.

"You can't kick me out." His face is turning red, and I know I'm hitting all his buttons.

"Actually, I can. I have the right to refuse business," I tap my foot up and down on the tile floor, "I don't need yours."

"Fine," he sputters, "Kai mentioned you were dating someone, and that it was a coworker. Since you don't tell us what is going on in your life, I wanted to come see for myself if he was telling the truth. Imagine my surprise to see you making out with someone considerably younger than you."

Of course, my brother let that slip. I wonder if that was before or after he cornered me about Xander meeting them. Most likely before, and he was trying to cover his ass when he made the proposal.

"Does it matter? Last time I checked I'm a grown woman, and able to do what I want. Besides, you and Mom don't make it easy to talk to y'all."

"That's beside the point."

"No, it really is," I pause for a second, "you know what, I can't do this." I grab one of the biggest bouquets we have out here right now and shove it in my dad's hands. "Here are the flowers for Mom. Please leave."

He acts like he wants to stay, but he must be able to sense my mood. With the flowers still in his hands, he marches out the door and into the fading light. I close the door behind him and lock it. I'm going to murder my brother.

I don't bother picking up the cleaning supplies on my way to the back of the shop. I'll come early in the morning and finish up. The audacity my father has to come up here to *check* on me. What the actual hell?

My entire body goes rigid when I look around the warehouse and don't see Xander anywhere. It looks like everyone left as soon as they could. Except one person, and it's not the person I thought it would be.

"So, that went well." Samantha is cleaning up the work tables and putting things where they go.

"You heard?" I should not have yelled like that while here.

"Yep," she nods, "Xander left right before the yelling began, but he looked like someone took his favorite toy away. Both sad and furious. Would you know anything about that?"

Ugh, I'm absolutely awful. "I made him leave before I got into with my dad. I didn't think he'd actually leave the whole shop, though."

If I'm being honest, I'm hurt he left. I thought what we have is bigger than this. Maybe it's best I learn this lesson with him now. When I let people in, they have the power to hurt me.

"My guess is it was for the best. He looked like he wanted to punch something, or someone, even though he was upset."

"Did he say anything?"

"That he'd see us tomorrow." She's finished putting everything away, and I hate the look she's giving me. "You know I love you, right?"

"Why do I feel like I'm about to get a lecture?"

"Kate, I love you like a sister. But you can't push Xander away when there's parts of your life you don't want him to see. I know you don't want him to meet your parents, but until you set clear boundaries with them, they are a part of your life. Compartmentalizing everything into neat little boxes won't end well."

"Says the person who claims they're going to murder

their neighbor every other morning." Rolling my eyes, I shake my head. She has a point, but I don't want to admit it.

"That's different. He's not someone I'm trying to have in my life forever. And I don't have to put up with his annoying self while I'm at work."

"Who said Xander was that for me?"

"Girl, you walk around here like a lovesick teenager. You may be denying it to yourself, but you've never really had a poker face. You are head over heels in love with Xander."

"No, I'm not." The rebuttal is quiet because she's right. As much as I've been saying it's nothing like that, my heart has been telling me differently.

"You've gotta stop lying to yourself." Sam turns out the light and heads to the door. "Are you locking up after I leave? Or, are you going now?"

"Oh, um, now." I walk out as she sets the alarm and wait for her to follow after me. "Did you see Kai before he left? Did he say anything?"

"No," she shakes her head, "said he was gonna grab some food with Viv. I'm guessing he had something to do with the little family reunion."

"That's putting it mildly." I head to my car grateful I drove today. I hear my bottle of wine calling me.

"I don't envy him when you see him."

My phone dings with a message and I pull it out of my pocket. "Speak of the devil."

KAI

You might want to head to Mom and Dad's.

I don't bother texting back I click on his profile and press call. The phone rings three times before he answers. At least he wasn't cowardly enough to send me to voicemail. "Why the hell would I go over there?"

"Well, Xander texted me for their address and said he had a last-minute delivery before he could clock out."

"And you gave it to him?" My voice is a shriek in the night. Sam stops on the way to her car and looks back at me. "In what world do you think I would have given Xander a delivery for their house? I mean seriously, Kai."

"I didn't think about that part until after I sent it to him." Regret fills his words. "I wasn't trying to pressure him into going over to meet them on his own."

"He's not going to meet them," I rub finger over my temple, "thanks to your little slip in conversation, Dad showed up at the shop not that long ago. And acted exactly how I thought he was going to. Xander is heading over there to defend my honor." Should I be completely pissed? Probably. Am I? No. He's doing one of those things I'm not used to. Taking care of me and making sure I don't have a ton piled on me, including emotional stress.

"Damn it," Kai mutters, "I'm already on my way over there. Want to meet me before Dad calls the cops?"

"Yeah, I'll be there in a few." I hang up the phone and glance over at Sam. "If I'm not here in the morning, just assume you'll have to bail me out of jail."

"Or Xander," she smirks, "I've got you either way. Be careful," she calls before getting in her car.

I'm definitely murdering my brother. All of this is his fault.

⁂

Xander must have waited a bit after getting the address from my brother. He's walking up the sidewalk to the front door. He must not have noticed me pull up. I get out of the car and gently close it behind me.

I should stop him, I know that. But I want to know what he plans on telling my dad. If the situation gets sketchy, I can always show up and handle it. My steps are silent as I follow along behind him, but stay just out of sight of the front door. Thank God my parents have decent landscaping that hides my actions.

Xander knocks on the door and I hide behind the tree. My brother isn't here yet and I'm glad because he would not be quite as stealthy. The porch light flicks on, and my dad is standing in the door way.

"Can I help you?" It takes him a second to realize who just knocked on his door and his eyes widen. "I don't want any trouble, son."

It annoys me that's the first thing that pops into his mind. But I guess I can see it from his point of view.

"I don't either, Sir," Xander replies, "but I am going to need you to stop talking to Kate the way you do. From what I've gathered from her, and Kai, you treat her drastically different than you do him. And based on the small interaction at the shop earlier, I'd agree."

My dad opens his mouth to respond, but Xander doesn't let him.

"Do you have any idea how incredible Kate is? She has her own business, friends that have been with her since they were kids, and booming clientele that will only use Whoopsie Daisy for their floral needs. Do you think that would be possible if she wasn't an amazing person? The way you've treated her has given her so many scars. She was terrified to meet my parents because she was worried they would be like you. She won't let anyone get close. She thinks being in a relationship means handing over control of herself and being belittled."

"That's not at all what's happened," Dad stammers.

"That's exactly how she feels, and it's your fault." He points his finger at my dad, coming within inches of actually touching his chest.

"Hey, man," Kai comes running up the sidewalk. When did he get here? I didn't even notice. "Maybe we can take this inside before someone calls the cops."

Damn. I can't let him go inside on his own. "I don't think that's necessary." I step out from behind the tree.

"What the hell is going on?" My dad's voice booms, filling the quiet street.

My feet carry me to Xander's side, and I slip my hand into his. "Everything he said is exactly how I feel."

"Why haven't you said anything before?" Dad's

hands go to his hips in defense. "It's not like you've ever been one to hold your tongue."

"Because it's not that easy when you're dealing with your own parents," I argue. "Y'all haven't exactly been warm and loving toward us." I point between me and Kai. "Not even to each other. How were we supposed to feel comfortable enough to come to you when something upset us?"

"That was never our intention," Dad says, confused as to why I would think that.

"Look, Dad," Kai interrupts, "it's late, and we've all had a long day. We'll revisit this conversation after we've all had a bit of time to cool off."

He's not wrong. "Bye, Dad," I wave to the man still standing on the porch. I'm surprised my mom didn't come out with all the commotion. As soon as we're down the path, I point at Kai, "You and I are going to have a discussion."

"I'm well aware," Kai says as he backs down the sidewalk.

Xander doesn't let go of my hand as I drag us down the driveway to my car. "How did you know I was here?"

"Kai called." I wait for a few moments until my dad goes back inside. "Why did you come over here? I was going to handle it."

He runs a hand through is hair and studies the ground. "Because I didn't like the way he was talking to you. That's not how I wanted to meet your dad earlier, and I thought if he understood how amazing you are, he'd at least ease up on you."

"I doubt that will happen, but thank you," I lean up and kiss him on the cheek, "even though I didn't need you to handle my battle."

"I know, but this is a sore spot for you. It would be hard either way. The least I could do is ease the burden some. How you go from here with your parents is your choice. But I couldn't let the conversation from earlier go without saying my piece."

"Want to get out of here?"

"Absolutely. That was actually kind of terrifying," he laughs, "you're place or mine."

"Mine, and don't bother trying to leave tonight. Hell, you might as well bring your stuff to my place."

"Are you sure? I don't want you to ask me to move in with you because you feel obligated."

"I'm positive. I love you, Xander, and I kind of can't sleep when you aren't there."

"Ah, so you're using me for sleep?"

"You're such a jerk," I take a step to move away from him, "of course, I'm not."

He pulls me back to him, and wraps his arms around me. "I love you, too. Hell, I'm pretty sure I've been in love with you since the first time I saw you."

"That's cree—" He cuts off my words with his lips.

xander

THERE'S A POUNDING on the door, and I'm unsure whether or not I should answer it. I mean, Kate asked me to move in, but I'm not entirely comfortable answering the door after my first night here.

Kate is in the shower, and I don't want whoever is at the door to wait, or leave. What if it's something important? It's not like I can act like I didn't hear them. The TV is on, and these walls aren't very thick. They know someone is home.

Setting down the remote, I stand from the couch. Hopefully, it's not Kate's parents because I feel like that isn't going to go over well. A night isn't long enough for them to cool down. Kate has experienced years of disappointment from there, it's going to take time.

I can hear the shower turn off as I open the front door, and I hope Kate gets dressed before she comes in here. Kai is standing there with coffee and donuts. At least he knows the way to his sister's heart.

"Oh, sorry. I didn't realize you'd be here." Kai looks nervously inside the apartment, "is my sister around?"

"Yeah, she's getting out of the shower." I open the door wider, "come in."

"Thanks. I didn't want to wait to get my tongue lashing from her. Knowing her, she'd draw it out for days just to make sure I'm as uncomfortable as possible." I close the door behind him.

He's not wrong. I've seen glimpses of how petty she can be. I don't wish that treatment on anyone. "I think she'll appreciate you coming with an offering. I'll go get her."

"Thanks, man." He sets the box of donuts on the coffee table and looks around, eyes rolling at the tree still up in the corner. Before I can move toward the hall, he says, "when I was hinting at you meeting our parents, I didn't mean for you to confront them. You have more balls than I ever could. Hell, the only reason my mom met Vivian when she did is because we ran into her at the holiday festival."

"It needed to be done, and I didn't appreciate the way your dad was talking to Kate when he showed up at the shop," I shrug it off as if it's no big deal. Truth be told, I was terrified. I fully expected the cops to show up, but I'm glad he heard me out.

"Either way, kudos to you."

Nodding I move down the hallway to the bedroom. Kate is standing by the bed in a robe, drying her hair. "Hey, um, your brother is in the living room."

She drops her towel and tightens her robe before

marching out of the room. I wonder for a split second if I should follow after her before I decide I probably should...for Kai's protection.

"You have some nerve showing up here this morning," Kate yells. I wince as the words ring out around the apartment. The neighbors have to be able to hear her.

"I'm come with gifts," Kai says quickly. He points to the box of donuts on the coffee table as I enter the living room.

"I don't care what you brought. What gave you the right to mention Xander to our parents? I told you numerous times I would tell them when I was ready. It was my choice to make, not yours. I don't have the picture perfect relationship that you have with them. They'll be lucky if I allow them to stay in my life after that stunt Dad pulled."

Kai jumps into the argument as she takes a breath, "I said I'm sorry. It slipped. I didn't do it intentionally. I also didn't tell Dad to go by the shop. I don't know why he did that."

"It doesn't matter," she shakes her head. "I basically kicked him out. But from now on, try to keep from slipping them information about me. If I want them to know, *I'll* tell them. Do you think you can handle that?"

Kai glances over his sister's shoulder at me. Little does he know, I won't be much help. "Um, I think so."

"Well, I thought you could before, and yet..."

"No," he stands taller. "I know I can. I promise I won't screw it up again, and I'll stop bugging you about Mom and Dad."

"Good. Now, I need to finish getting ready for work." She turns back to the hallway.

"I'm just going to leave all this right here," he sets the coffee he was holding on the table. "I'll see y'all at the shop."

He doesn't wait for a response and rushes out the door. I don't blame him. Kate is the most amazing woman I've ever met, but she can be intimidating. I'm also glad I don't have siblings.

"Want me to bring his peace offering to the room while you get ready?"

"That would great," she calls back. "Hopefully we won't have any more issues about my parents."

For Kai's safety, I hope not. Work is going to be interesting today.

Waking up next to Kate is something I'm already passed used to. Except when I roll over, she isn't in bed. What the hell? It's unlike her to wake up before me. I pull the comforter off me and grab my sweats from the floor.

"Kate? Are you here?" My voice rings out in the apartment. It's silent except for some thuds coming from the kitchen. What is she doing? I follow the sounds and see her pulling out the baking dish I used to make her dinner. "What are you doing?"

"Cooking you breakfast?" She's unsure of herself. She points to the can of cinnamon rolls. "It's not much. But how badly can I screw these up?"

"I'm sure they will be delicious." We haven't talked about what happened the other night at her parents. She had girl's night and the past two days we've been swamped at work. This is the last Saturday we'll be able to sleep in for a while.

"How are your parents handling you staying over here?" She asks as she sprays the pan. "I hope they aren't angry with me."

"Not at all." Which is weird. I thought they'd take the news of me moving out badly. "I think they're happy they can be all lovey dovey without me being there to complain."

"Think of all the making out they'll be doing all over the kitchen."

"Blegh, why would you put that image in my mind? That's pure evil, woman."

Kate points the can of cinnamon rolls at me. "Firstly, don't call me woman," she opens the casing and puts them in the dish, "secondly, at least they love each other."

"Speaking of," this isn't really territory I want to cross first thing in the morning, but something has to be said, "what are you going to do about your parents?"

She doesn't answer me immediately. "I'm not sure. I know I need to talk to them, but I think I need to do it on my own."

"Understandable." As much as I want to be there for her if things go sideways, I know she'll be able to handle it. Maybe they can really reconcile and rebuild their relationship. "Don't forget to set the timer," I say as she slides the cinnamon rolls into the oven.

"I know." She studies the oven for a moment before picking up her phone.

"What are you doing?"

"Setting a timer. I don't know how to work the one on the stove."

That's something I'll have to show her later if she'll be cooking more often. "What do you want to do today? It looks like this is our last free weekend for the foreseeable future."

"I don't know. Maybe go to the bar? I heard there's supposed to be a decent band there tonight."

It's not a bad idea. I like live music as much as the next person. "But that's not until tonight. What are we going to do the rest of the day?"

She stalks toward me. Her eyes never leaving mine. "After we eat breakfast, you're going to join me in the bedroom. I don't plan on leaving the apartment until later tonight. Does that sound good?"

I pull her to me, and lift her up. "That sounds like the best idea you've had all morning."

She giggles as I walk backward toward the hallway. "What about the cinnamon rolls?"

"Screw breakfast."

With a poke to my side, I release her. "That's what you think, but I don't want the fire department showing up when the smoke detectors go off."

"Fine," I follow her back into the kitchen, "but I propose breakfast in bed."

"I can get down with that." Huh, that didn't take much convincing.

✻

The bar parking lot is mostly full when we get there. We'll be lucky to get a standing table. Not that I plan on spending a ton of time at the table. If I have my way, we'll be on the dance floor the majority of the evening.

I drop Kate off at the front door before parking my car. I find a spot at the very back of the lot. I've never seen it this full. Even when they have live music. I lock up the car and hurry to the front door. She's waiting for me just inside the door.

"Good news," Kate says as she leans into me, "Delilah says there's about to be an empty high top, and we've got dibs."

"We aren't dancing?" That's the main reason I come here when I do.

"Yes, but not until after I eat." Her stomach growls at the mention of food. "I'm starving."

"That tends to happen when you keep me in bed all day."

Delilah gags behind the podium. "You guys know you're not as quiet as you think you are, right?"

"Oh, sorry." Kate's cheeks redden.

Delilah peeks around the corner. "Looks like the table is ready. Do you need menus?"

"Nope," Kate grins, "I already know what we're

getting." She grabs my hand and pulls me toward the table Delilah pointed out.

"You know, you and your brother have a knack for ordering food for people. Is that a hereditary thing?"

"I don't think that's possible." She gets into the chair and I push her in until she's closer to the table. "We just know good food, and everyone should eat it."

"If you say so." I move around to the other side of the table. I see a few couples sprinkled at tables around the room. Most of them are sitting side by side. That feels weird to me. How are you supposed to look at the person you're with if they aren't in front of you. Unless they don't talk on dates which is weird in itself.

When the waiter comes, Kate orders us wings. I swear sometimes it's like they are the same person. No wonder they get along and fight at the same time. Before the waiter can leave, she asks, "Do you know who's playing tonight?"

"We aren't supposed to say anything, but it's Crooked Halo."

"I knew there was another reason Spencer and Tiffany were in town," Kate claps her hands together, "I love these guys."

I know their music. I'm a fan, but it's not a band I expect to play here very often. "I guess this means no dancing."

Kate reaches her hand across the table and pats mine. "We can dance during the slow songs."

There is that. The waiter brings our food, but our drinks haven't come yet. I'm about to get up and ask what the holdup is, but that guy I saw with Kate that first night comes to our table, drinks in hand.

"Sorry about this, guys. Joan was supposed to work tonight but the kids are sick," he shakes his head and sighs. "I told her they are teenagers and capable of taking care of their basic necessities when they're sick, but she won't listen."

"Thanks, Eric," Kate grins, "be happy she's there for them. There are a lot of parents who aren't."

"True," he nods in agreement, "hey, do happen to have any friends looking for a rental? Joan and I are getting a house, and Carlos asked me to put out some feelers."

"Actually, I might be interested," Kate surprises me with her answer. She made it clear she doesn't like to do the maintenance in an actual house. What angle is she playing here?

"I'll tell Carlos. And it'll be about a month or so. We're waiting to sign a contract," he taps the table. "Let me know if y'all need anything."

"We will." The words come out of my mouth, trying to get him to leave the table. Once he's gone, my focus is on Kate. "Since when are you interested in his house?"

"Since I know it's coming up for rent, and as much as I love apartment living, we'll need a bigger space to host friends."

"So, you really meant what you said the other night?" Confirmation is the one thing I need right now.

"About what? You moving in and not leaving? Yes.

We talked about that this morning." She takes a bite of her wing.

"No, not that part. When you said you loved me?" Surely, she wouldn't ask me to move in if she didn't feel some sort of emotion toward me.

"Have you been wondering that this whole time?" Her mouth opens wide in shock.

"A little." Yeah, my parents may be the poster children for a happy couple, but I still need the assurance.

"Yes, I love you." She slides out of her chair and walks around to my side of the table. "Why would you think otherwise?"

"I don't know," I shrug. "It could have been one of those middle of battle word slips."

"Love isn't something you accidentally say. It's something you feel." She leans her head against my chest and sighs. "I just happen to feel it when I'm with you. It took Samantha getting mean with me for me to realize it. I was heading to your place to share my revelation with you. Then all hell broke loose and you decided to storm my parent's house."

"That wasn't entirely my fault." I wince at the memory of confronting Kate's dad. "But it needed to be said."

"And that right there is why I fell all the way in love with you. Our relationship may not be convenient with work and everything else, but I can't deny I love you."

"Love you, too." I bend down and give her a quick kiss on the lips. "Now finish eating so we'll be ready to dance during the slow songs."

epilogue

THERE ARE MOVING boxes scattered around the apartment. Each one carefully labeled. Most people would have tons of cardboard boxes filled with kitchen utensils, but Kate's only takes up two. Even after I moved in, she refused to buy more cookware. She said that would be the first thing we did together when we got a more permanent place to live. Honestly, I think she's getting tired of apartment life.

"Hey, what are you doing in here?" Kate comes up behind me and puts her arms around my waist. I jump at the touch because she keeps poking me and it's driving me up the wall.

"Making sure all the dishes are in boxes. Did you get the rest of the bedroom packed up?"

"Yep, everything is ready for the movers." She lets go of me and backs away. She pulls her phone out of her pocket and glances at the time. "They should be here in ten minutes. Is it weird that I'm excited about this move?"

"I don't think so." I leave the kitchen and head toward the living room. More boxes fill the space and the couch. I really hope these movers are prepared to carry that thing down all those stairs. Though, I'm sure we can figure out some sort of pulley system. Moving furniture down narrow stairs is not my idea of a good time.

"Is that because you're moving with me?"

"Nope. It's because it's a new adventure." I go through the boxes to make sure they are taped securely. "One I can't wait to get started with you."

"Ah, you really do love me."

"I didn't realize that was up for debate."

"It wasn't. I just like seeing you all ooey gooey." She comes toward me once again, this time cornering me against a wall.

"You realize we have a high likelihood of being like my parents when we're older, right? We'll embarrass the hell out of any kids we may or may not have."

"True," she laughs, "for the time being, I'm okay with not having kids. No offense to those that have them, but I'm good."

She leans closer to me, and has me pinned between her and the wall. Her lips are inches away from mine when the doorbell rings. Life with Kate is going to be interesting, and I can't wait to live it with her. Even her parents are showing up to help us unpack. That's a step in the right direction, but it's going to take more than a few weeks for them to mend all their broken feelings toward each other. But...it's a start. And I can't wait to see what this new life brings the both of us.

*

Who knew being an "adult" would be so tedious? It's been hours of looking at houses. This whole process seems much easier in movies and TV shows. Most of those people find their dream house in a matter of minutes. I've been at this for weeks.

"Can we stop for food?" Kate whines from the back seat. "I'm starving."

"We still have three more houses on the list." I drive right past a few restaurants. "I want to see what the outside looks like before I get in touch with the realtor."

"And we can still do that," Kate argues. "But if I don't eat soon, it's not going to be pretty."

Why did I think bringing my best friends would be a good idea? They've found something wrong with every house we've looked at. It wouldn't normally bug me, but everything they've pointed out has been minor. It's like they have a vendetta against me buying a house.

"Fine, where would you like to eat?"

"Somewhere that serves booze."

Leave it to Kate to want to find a sit down place that will take longer than a drive thru.

"What about you Emily? Is there anywhere in partic-ular you'd like to go?"

She stares out the passenger window for a bit before responding. "It doesn't matter to me."

Of course she'd be neutral. It's the position she usually takes when Kate and I can't come to an agreement. I don't hold it against her, though. Kate and I are both headstrong. We're also petty for no reason. It's a wonder we've been able to stay friends this long.

A restaurant comes into view, and I ease off the gas to turn into the parking lot. It's a place we've come to before, and the only reason I decided on it is because the lot is virtually empty. "Fine. We'll eat."

"Yes," Kate throws her hand up in victory. Her knuckles hit the roof, and she yelps. "Ow. I forgot for a second that we're in a vehicle."

"Are you sure drinking is a good idea?" I put the car in park and step outside. Once she opens the door, I keep going. "If you forgot you were in a car, what hope do I have that you'll be able to pay attention to the houses?"

"Please," she scoffs, "you act like I can't handle my booze. I'll totally be fine."

Like I believe that. She's going to get full on food, have a couple of margaritas, and take a nap in the backseat. It's been happening this way since we were in college. Now, we're officially grown. Or, that's what we keep telling ourselves.

"Fine, let's get inside so we can drive by these last few houses before heading home."

"I don't know why you want to move out of the apartment anyway," Kate grumbles as we enter the restaurant. "It's not like we're piled on top of each other. And we always have a good time."

That's the thing, though. We're *always* together. We

see each other at work, at home, and when we go out for drinks. I love my friends dearly, but I need some space. And it's finally within my grasp since the flower shop has become a staple for our town.

I get why she doesn't want me to move out. Aside from her brother, she didn't have the upbringing Emily and I did. We weren't treated the way her parents treated her.

But after years of sharing a room with my sister, then a dorm room, and now an apartment. I'm ready to stretch my limbs and be on my own. I don't know how to explain that to her, though.

"Just think of all the things you can do with an empty room."

"You know," she nods, "you're right."

Emily shakes her head and laughs, "No, you don't get it all to yourself. We're splitting it down the middle. Fifty-fifty."

"Buzzkill," Kate pouts. They can duke that out on their own after I've found a house I like. At least she's no longer making jabs at me.

"This is it!" I jump up and down, clapping my hands.

"Is that a smile?" Emily steps in front of me to study my expression. "Kate, come here, I think Sam is broken."

Kate rushes to us after poking around in the kitchen. I don't know why. We've been friends practically our whole lives and I've never once seen her pick up a cooking utensil.

"I think you're right." She presses against my shoulder to see if I'm real. "Who are you? And, what have you done with Samantha?"

"You know," I stop my celebration, "you aren't that funny."

"Please, I'm hilarious." She places a hand over her chest as if she's offended. "But, I agree. This house is perfect for you. Well, except for the fact she'll have neighbors."

"We have neighbors now," Emily points out. "The plus side is she won't be sharing a wall with any of them."

Kate whirls on Emily. "Don't tell me you're considering moving out now, too. I can't lose both of my friends to adulthood at the same time."

She blames it on that, but I know it's because she doesn't want to lose her sense of family. Because that's what me and Emily are to her...family.

"I'm not going anywhere. I want to have a big nest egg before I even consider it."

"You mean, your parents want you to have a ton of money in savings before you take that step." I add to the conversation. "They probably have an entire spreadsheet set up for you, don't they?"

"I'm not answering that." Emily juts her chin in the air. I'm right, I know it. Their relationship is almost as weird as Kate's with her parents. The difference is

Emily's mom and dad want her to have the stability they have. It comes from a place of love.

"So, we can put in an offer?" The realtor asks once there's a quiet moment between the three of us. Who knows what she probably thinks of us. We're so comfortable around each other we sometimes forget how to act when other people are around.

"Most definitely." I spin around the living room, imagining how I'm going to place my furniture. It'll be nice having total control over the decoration. I don't have to make compromises with roommates.

"Excellent," the realtor grins. "We'll go with your minimum offer, and if they deny that, we'll go up from there until we hit your max. Is that okay with you?"

"Absolutely." I squeal, and kind of freak myself out. I'm not used to being this happy over something. "How long will it take?"

"It's hard to tell, but I'll try to get the sale closed as quickly as possible." She glances at the legal pad in her hand. "In no time I'll be handing you the keys."

"This is so exciting."

"I think we should celebrate." Kate whoops.

"It's not official, yet." I mutter.

"Who cares?" Emily butts in, "you found a place that none of us have an issue with. It calls for celebration."

This is why I love my friends, and why they are all I'll ever need.

acknowledgments

It goes without saying that writing a book takes a village. I wouldn't be where I am without my support system. I love creating new characters in my little world for you to devour

Steph, thanks for always being my cheerleader when I need to get the words in. If it wasn't for your livestreams, I don't know that this book would have been finished. One day we'll get to hang out in person instead of online.

Wee One...you kept me on track. The periodic bugging me to make sure I'm writing is exactly the push I needed when I'd rather binge watch my shows. Never change!

Hubs & Boy Child, thank you for not talking to me when y'all knew I was writing. That's seriously the best gift ever. And Baby E, you are the cutest distraction when I need a break. Being your gamaw is the biggest honor.

To my Patrons, Cindy & Stephanie. Your unwavering support means more than you could ever know.

Readers, bloggers, and anyone else who picks up my books. Thank you! You have no idea how much you reading my words means to me. I couldn't do this without your support. Your excitement keeps me going.

Do you want to meet more of the characters in Asheville? You can check out my books here. Or, scan the QR code to find out what some of the other residents of this small town are up to.

about the author

Katrina Marie lives in the Dallas area with her husband, two children, grand baby, and fur baby. She is a lover of all things geeky and nerdy. When she's not writing you can find her at her daughter's sporting events, playing with the grand, or curled up reading a book.

You can find Katrina Marie online in the following places:

Sign up for my newsletter: https://www.subscribepage.com/KatrinaMarieNewsletter

Website: katrinamarieauthor.com

facebook.com/katrinamarieauthor

x.com/katmarieauthor

instagram.com/katrinamarieauthor

bookbub.com/profile/katrina-marie

pinterest.com/katrinamarieauthor

tiktok.com/@katrinamarieauthor

patreon.com/katrinamarie